DREAD MURDER

In   Mearns, a veteran   is the guardian of Windsor Cas . Wor ng with the resourceful Sergeant Denny, the pair maintain a cool façade behind which they go about their duties quietly and unnoticed.

Unnoticed, that is, until the day Major Mearns receives a parcel containing a gruesome surprise: a pair of severed human legs. Legs that belonged to a fellow soldier. Mearns and Denny decide to investigate the murder, enrolling the help of a precocious young runaway, Charlie. But soon they find themselves up against all manner of obstacles and danger.

With more butchered body parts turning up and the number of deaths rising, the amateur investigators soon find themselves up to their necks in corruption and intrigue.

DREAD MURDER

A Major Mearns Mystery

Gwendoline Butler

WINDSOR

PARAGON

First published 2006
by
Allison & Busby
This Large Print edition published 2007
by
BBC Audiobooks Ltd by arrangement with
Allison & Busby

Hardcover ISBN: 978 1 405 61514 3
Softcover   ISBN: 978 1 405 61515 0

British Library Cataloguing in Publication Data available

Printed and bound in Great Britain by
Antony Rowe Ltd., Chippenham, Wiltshire

ACKNOWLEDGEMENTS

I wish to thank John Kennedy Melling for his technical advice, especially on the 19th century theatre and particularly on the amazing life and management of the Theatre Royal, Windsor of Henry Thornton.

CHAPTER ONE

The town of Windsor was wrapped in mist; it came up from the river to cover the town and the Castle on the hill.

In his set of rooms deep in the heart of the Castle, Major Mearns sat over his breakfast, drinking hot tea while he read *The London Times*.

'Drat the dust,' said Mearns, shaking a powder of grey from the papers and, indeed, from his breakfast as well. He could hear the crashing and banging of stonemasons so he knew from whence came the dirt.

The Castle was being restored by the new King, who had found the edifice crumbling from a century of neglect; the King, who had a perceptive eye, was determined to return it to grandeur.

But for the lesser souls like the Major and Denny who lived in the Castle, it meant noise and dirt. The men worked harder when the King was in residence, as he was at present, so that all the residents were grateful when he returned to Buckingham Palace, which he was also restoring, and the Castle quietened down.

The smell of the dust kept bringing back an episode he would like to forget. A woman, of course. 'All the worst troubles came from the female sex' was the Major's view. A duchess, no less. She was strongly suspected, so the message came from Mr Pitt's staff, of having poisoned two people. 'Do not let her do the same in Windsor' was the message that came with her.

In this, alas, he had not succeeded. 'She got

1

away with murder,' he said to himself, shaking his head as he always did when he thought of Madame La Duchesse. Then she had curtsied to the old Queen and gone off.

But where had she got to? That was the real mystery to interest the gossips.

Mearns went back to reading with a sigh, brushing a spatter of dust from his hair with his hands. To be sure all this work might rid the Castle of its bugs—a persistent and prolific population.

It was not his copy of the newspaper, as it was an expensive item which he preferred to read but not to buy. Sergeant Denny, his friend and supporter in his business as Watcher in the Castle, read the paper after him. They were both slow, careful readers, so this took some time. Then the paper would be folded, ironed and delivered to His Majesty King George IV—not so long ago his Royal Highness, the Prince Regent, but still a drunken layabout even if a man of excellent taste in clothes and pictures. Not to mention women.

Mearns and Denny knew that the King rose late, very late, so that there would be no early call for his newspaper—if indeed he read it at all, which both men doubted. They were not admirers of His Majesty, although they appreciated his choice in wine, bottles of which sometimes found their way to their table. As soldiers both, they preferred rum or whisky, but wine would do. They had fought side by side in some of the wars against Napoleon, pillaging and sampling the wines as they went through.

They had served in Wellington's army in various quiet ways so that when William Pitt looked around for someone to keep a watchful eye on the

Royal household (an unfortunate necessity because of Mad King George's illness, his wife's foreign relations and the behaviour of the then Prince of Wales) these two got the task.

Watchers, spies, guardians—call them what you will; they did their work quietly and with such tact that they made friends in the Castle household rather than enemies.

That is, if they were noticed at all. Somehow they contrived to be just a bit of background furniture.

William Pitt was dead, Napoleon was dead, the mad old King was dead; but these two Watchers were still here in the Castle, reporting now to Lord Castlereagh. There would always be someone or something for the Watchers to report on while King George IV and Queen Caroline (only divorced and never crowned, but now on the scene again) lived, and also later, if Mearns and Denny themselves should survive, when the young Princess Charlotte grew up if heredity was anything to go by. The two men did a good job.

'And if we hadn't known how to behave ourselves, then we would never have survived the wars. Not noticed is how you want to be in a war if you are to get through it,' Denny had observed sagely as he speared a slice of ham on to his plate.

'The one thing we can say about the Castle is that the pay is poor but the food is good.'

'So it is,' agreed the Sergeant. It was his duty to go to the kitchens, of which there were many, each having their own functions, and bring back their food. He had always done this—in Portugal, in Spain, and through France. He was a natural scavenger. The Major remained aloof from all this as officers do not do such things, but it was his function to point Denny in the direction of the foods they both wanted. Never ask how he got his information; it was part of being a Watcher.

'Brew another pot, Denny.' He watched while the Sergeant warmed the metal pot, put in the tea leaves, then waited for them to infuse. In the poor household in which he had grown up, Denny had seen the tea leaves used, and used again. He felt rich now in being able to be lavish. After a minute or two he poured a cup for the Major, waited for Mearns to drink and nod his approval, then drank himself. It was a ritual the two went into every morning.

'I read in *The Times* that the King's health is improving, and that he has had a "peaceful rest". "His Majesty is making a good recovery and we shall soon see him restored to active life." We know better than that. Not while he drinks the way he does. That's his sickness.'

'Active enough in some ways,' commented Denny. 'Too active. You can hear his shouting and swearing down the stairs and two floors away. Screaming like a dog with fits. 'Tis a fit.'

Mearns nodded gravely. 'Madness, madness. Like his father.'

'Mindy says that he is not so violent; not biting the doctors and kicking all who come near him so bad that they have to bind him up in a kind of dead suit.' Thus had the mad old King been treated. His son had a touch of his madness—all his sons had—but mildly, mildly.

Charlotte Minden, now more fondly called Mindy by her friends, had come to the Castle as a very young, frightened girl—not even sure of her

4

own name. She was to act as a maidservant to Miss Fanny Burney, the author, who was then In Waiting upon the Queen. Fanny called her Charlotte, and Fanny's father, Dr Burney, had added the name 'Minden', after a famous battle. As Mindy had taken root in the castle and matured and flourished, she grew into a handsome woman. Meanwhile, Fanny had continued writing her novels, knowing her own success as a married woman. In time Fanny found that the trials of attending on the Queen were too exacting and exhausting, and so she had fled from the Castle. But the sturdier Charlotte had stayed and prospered.

Mindy had not married, although she had not wanted for suitors. The Major had watched the girl grow into a woman; he thought of his affection as paternal, but lately he had acknowledged some warmer emotion growing there.

Could you fall in love at his age? He was still denying it to himself; but Denny, watching him, knew he had. Sergeant Denny, himself, had a happy and good-natured lover in the town. Twice widowed, she had said that that was marriage and death enough. 'Never ask me to marry you,' she had said to Denny. 'For I'd say "No".'

It might be a lie, but Denny told the odd lie himself, and in fact had a wife in Cripplegate, London, whom he had not seen for years (and possibly some others elsewhere). For all he knew, she was looking for him. Not dead, for she had vowed to haunt him if necessary and he had never seen her ghost—although there were so many ghosts in the Castle that he might not have noticed one more.

Mindy, of course, was different, as was the Major. Not liars, either of them, although they might be haunted.

What was doubtful was Mindy's own feelings. She loved them both, but was it the love that the Major wanted? As for himself, Denny had no hopes.

In these same years, a revolution had swept over France while, without a revolution, the nature of society in Britain was changing too. Britain was slowly turning into an industrial nation with new riches in new regions: Wales and the industrial north of England, rich in coal and iron, and busy with weaving cloth for the workers and for the new markets across the seas.

Political life, too, had changed, with the sickness of the old King, and the disinclination of the young one to be King—a factor which, together with the rising wealth and power of the middle classes, served to enhance the House of Commons while slowly depreciating the importance of land and farming.

Not much of this was felt in Windsor Castle, except for the illness of the mad old King—which had troubled the whole household, including Mindy whose closeness to the old Queen and the unmarried Princesses showed her their troubles at close hand.

'She's grown into a handsome woman,' said the Major, dwelling fondly on Mindy.

'Oh, you would notice that,' said Sergeant Denny to himself.

'She will catch someone's eye and be off to be a wife.'

'I daresay,' Denny replied to the Major.

'In fact I've heard that one of the coachmen, Joe Hilly, has his eye on her.'

'He's only got half an eye,' said Denny.

'Aye, his left eye does move around a mite,' agreed the Major.

'She deserves better than Hilly; he smells of horses.'

'So she does, so she does.'

'I reckon Mindy knows her own value.'

Mearns nodded, before going back to his breakfast. 'He is a warm man, is Hilly. You can do well in the stables if you know your business.'

It was true that a man with his eyes open could make a profit out of being a royal servant in the household of King George III, and his successor for that matter.

The subject of making money reminded him of a friend. 'Mr Pickettwick is back today,' he remarked to Denny.

'So he is.'

Samuel Pickettwick was a retired businessman experiencing good circumstances who divided his time between London and Windsor. He himself never mentioned money; he had no need to do so, for he exuded comfort and prosperous living. In any case, the Major—who had his own way of checking—had found out that he owned a manufactory in Manchester as well as several emporia in the poorer parts of London that sold any cotton or silk that failed in the richer world. A sensible arrangement, thought Mearns: sell to the poor what the rich don't want.

Mr Pickettwick's business was now run by his nephew who remained in London, living in Gray's Inn Road. Major Mearns had his own reasons for believing the nephew not to be a nephew at all, but a bastard son.

Mr Pickettwick was one of the Major's sources of London gossip, all of which was grist to his mill. There was a tacit agreement between them to exchange information: London items from one side and Court and Cabinet tips from the other. Probably neither party trusted the other completely but, that said, they enjoyed each other's company.

'Nice to see the old boy again,' said Denny, who licked no one's boots and had his own notion of 'Mr P', as he called him. 'We must give him a din-din. He likes his grub.'

'And his drink.'

'That's right, Major,' said Denny with a grin. Mearns had an officer's rank, won in war, and Denny was a Sergeant, but there was an equality of status between them—Denny was the Major's other self.

There was a sharp double rap on the door.

'Could be Tommy Traddles . . . I heard he was around looking for you the other day, but couldn't find you.'

'He could have found me fast enough if he'd really looked,' said the Major. 'I'm glad he didn't find me—wanted to borrow some money, I expect. And you never get it back.' The Major went back to his reading.

'He spat at me last time I saw him,' reminisced Denny. 'And dang me if I know why.'

'No, he's not a nice man,' said Mearns, 'but he has sent more felons that deserved it to the gallows than you and I have.' Traddles was a Watcher and a Searcher who worked for the most important

London Magistrates. He worked for anyone who would pay him; he had certainly worked for Mearns, identifying and bringing in those suspected of crimes.

There came another rap on the door.

The Major raised his eyes from the paper. 'Open it, Denny . . .'

But even as the Sergeant moved towards the door, it swung open and, not Traddles, but Charlotte Minden stood there, a long, striped shirt hanging over one arm.

'You were long enough opening the door.'

Denny shot towards her.

'Here, Denny, here is the shirt I mended for you, and it is time you got another.' Denny murmured that he could not afford it.

'Well, get that Mr Pickettwick to give you one cheap—he sells them, I believe. He sent one to the King and the King said it would do as a nightshirt, but no more.' Mindy gave a huge sigh and sat down. 'If there is tea or coffee there, give me a cup. Such a night we have had of it.'

A cup, as big as a bowl, blue and white, was filled and handed to her.

'The King?' queried Major Mearns. 'Bad with the drink again, is he?'

Mindy took a long draught of tea. 'He has never been well, takes no notice of the doctors; he'll go like his father, but this night was beyond anything.' She finished her tea then put the cup down where Denny refilled it.

Taller now, slim and handsome, she was hardly the girl any more who had come to Windsor to work with Miss Fanny Burney (with whom she still corresponded). She wore a simple shift-like dress

9

with an apron tied around it; but it became her, as she well knew it did. She slipped her shawl from her shoulders.

'I believe the Queen, his mother, will leave Windsor and go to Kew. She is so cross with her son and he does not make her welcome.'

'Will you go?'

'I don't know yet. I may stay to be with Princess Adelaide. Lady Severn will stay. But the other Princesses will go with the Queen if she goes.'

'And his Majesty?'

'He will stay behind with his six keepers—or "Men" as they are called.'

Denny leaned against the window which looked out upon a covered way and then down to a small courtyard. 'His Majesty was very noisy again all yesterday.'

'He attacked his wife again last night,' said Mindy bluntly. 'Everyone in the Castle will know, so it's no secret . . . He does not want to take up his part as a husband, but thinks he should be with her to get a son. Queen Charlotte says she has a disgust of him.'

'Understandable,' said Mearns.

'Now when the old Queen retires, two of her German ladies and several of the Princesses go with her and stay with her until the King leaves . . . But last night, divorced or not, he wouldn't have any of it, or tried not to, and he attacked her. She should not have come back to the Castle. She liked Blackheath, but she was tempted.'

'You saw him?'

'Heard the screams and the noise . . . Lady Lorimer saw. And the doctors—they rushed in. Lady Lorimer says that Dr Willis and his helpers wrapped him up again in a kind of shroud so that he couldn't move—not a finger. They did it with the old King, you know. To think of it all happening again.'

'Henry VIII would have had their heads off for that,' remarked the Major.

Mindy finished her drink. 'I must go.' She wrapped her shawl around her. 'You must never say. All is secret.'

Except from Lord Castlereagh.

'It looks cold out there,' said Denny from his window perch.

Although it was still early morning, he could see people moving around in the courtyard. He knew most of them by sight, men and women both. This was one of his uses to Major Mearns; he never forgot a face.

He watched Mindy's graceful, strong figure swing out of sight. She had learnt how to bargain for a good wage from the Queen's household since Miss Burney had departed. The Queen could be generous, even handing on clothes that had served their time. The shawl, for instance, that Mindy was wearing that morning had probably started life over Royal shoulders.

He turned to the Major. 'Looks peaceful out there.'

'That's how I like it.' Like most old soldiers, they preferred a quiet life. 'Well—to work! What is it today?'

'I will take our tray back to the kitchens and talk to Barber; he always knows what is going on. If the Queen is off to Kew, it would be best to know for sure.'

'Do so,' Mearns nodded. 'And let him know we

are short of ale. After that, if it proves the Queen is on the move, then you might ride over to Kew and make our dispositions there.'

Denny nodded. 'And what will you be doing?' he thought to himself. 'Reading the King's paper and smoking your pipe?'

Mearns read his thoughts. 'The King can have his paper back. I will deliver it myself.'

'Not to him in person?'

'He won't be awake. No—in the tray to his dressing room. And then I will return here to write my report and get it sent off. Lord Tom is Messenger this week and I can trust him to deliver it.'

Lord Tom was not a peer, nor the son of one, but a rider from the stables who was sent on commissions by the Household. His name was one of those jokes that big households, like big families, spawn; his real name had been forgotten, but 'Duke' came into it somewhere. As the Major knew all the sins and crimes of everyone living in the Royal Household—knew of their lies, thefts, adulteries and even murders—someone he trusted with an important errand was not likely to betray him.

He knew in this instance that Lord Tom had killed an officer in the wars recently concluded. An unpleasant officer; a coward and a bully. But it would have been a shot in the head for Lord Tom and no more heard about him if he had been discovered. Even now, with victory and peace declared, it would have prevented him getting a job in the Royal stables, despite his skills with horses and guns.

The Major speculated that it had been some

letters found in his victim's pocket that had eased Lord Tom's way into the stables, but on this there was silence.

'And what do they all know about you, Sir?' Denny had asked humbly at the beginning of their working relationship.

'Nothing,' the Major had replied in a sad voice. 'There is nothing to know.'

This Denny did not believe.

After delivering the tray back to Barber, who, for once, was not informative, Denny took himself off for his usual early morning walk—which was in part a pleasure to him and in part a duty. He did not always take the same path because he must not be expected; but he always looked about him with observant eyes, ever noting and checking. This power of reading a scene had been invaluable to him as a soldier, saving his life more than once.

He walked out of the immediate Castle grounds towards the Great Park; then he debated whether to walk ahead or swing left to go through Shaw's Farm and then push into the Park. He must be brisk, anyway, as the Major would be waiting for his daily report. The Major had never got over his military way of expecting a succinct report, and quick too.

The park was heavily wooded, reminding him that this was once the hunting ground of the first Norman kings. Not an imaginative man, Denny did not waste much thought on the Normans. They hunted for food—no need for King George to do that; but the monarch enjoyed a ride himself when fit, and he still went out when he could escape his doctors, riding until the men of his Household were exhausted.

Denny looked about him, then decided to take a path through dense bushes and trees. He walked down through a leafy dell. He slowed his pace; he sniffed. He smelt death. Pushing his way through the bushes, he stopped suddenly. At his feet was a pool of blood. It was a kind of basin in the ground which was lined with dried leaves so hard and dense that the blood had not drained away.

Or not as yet, he thought—but soon it would, becoming thick and sticky.

Keeping his feet clear, he circled the bloody area. But there was nothing to see except the blood. He considered what he had seen as he walked back to the Castle.

Mearns was in his room, at his table, writing.

Denny spoke at once and bluntly: 'I have come across a pool of blood in the Park.'

Mearns barely raised his head from his writing. 'The remains of a fox's kill,' he said without interest.

Denny rapped on the table and stared Mearns in the eye. 'You and I have seen plenty of blood. We know how it falls. This is no blood from a fox's kill. Too much blood, and it would have fallen in pear-shaped drops, with a smear as the dead animal was dragged away.'

The Major stood up. 'We must look around, Denny.'

All the time there was a parcel on its way to be delivered to Major Mearns.

A dead weight, he joked when it was handed over to him.

*　　　*　　　*

14

The London to Windsor Coach arrived on time in the late afternoon. It stopped in the Market Square in sight of the Castle; the High Street ran into the Square. Here the coach stopped in front of The Royal George, the big inn which was its staging post before going on to Ascot.

The coachman climbed down, slashing his whip in the air. 'On time.' Punctual to the half-hour, this was promptness enough. The clock was not watched to the minute. With horse, hills and foul weather, you took what came.

The passengers descended from the coach, each one stiff and cold, glad to have arrived. The first to disembark was a woman. She was young and sprightly; she leapt down onto the paving stones, waved goodbye to the coachman and sped away.

'Goodbye, Miss Fairface,' the coachman called. She was an actress, about to perform in the new play at the Theatre Royal.

The three men who next appeared were slower, especially a plump, well-furred man to whom the others gave way.

'After you, Mr Pickettwick.'

The coachman touched his hat and pocketed his tip. 'Thank you, Sir.' He shook Mr Pickettwick's hand. Then he began to turn the coach in the direction of the stables where he would change the horses.

'Stop, stop,' cried Mr Pickettwick. 'Miss Tux is not out yet.'

Miss Tux. Tall, thin, more bone than flesh, bonneted and shawled, she was at the moment being lowered out of the coach by her maidservant who had a firm grip from behind on her elbows. 'Now don't pull away, Miss, or I'll drop you in the mud.'

'Libby, Libby, handle me gently,' a high, old voice was wailing.

Miss Tux was deposited, upright, on the ground, with Libby still holding on.

'Come along now, Miss Tux; let me take you in and see you get a little refreshment. A hot one, I advise. Mulled wine is good. And your chair is coming . . . I think I see the men pulling it up the hill now.'

In a low voice to one of his fellow travellers, Pickettwick explained: 'A lady of some substance in the town . . .'

There was one other passenger on the coach, and as it lumbered round to the stables, he poked his head over the top where he had been sitting.

'So you're still there, you little varmint,' growled the coachman.

'Coming down, don't you fear. Frozen, I am.' It was a young voice, full of spirit. The lad was small, with a shock of dark hair and an expressive face.

'Took a free ride, you did, young 'un. What's your name?'

'Charlie.'

'Right, Charlie, so you can pay for your ride by helping me with the horses.' The coachman's voice was gruff, but he was worried about the youngster. 'Do it well and there might be a penny or two for you.'

'Oh thank you, Sir.' Charlie sneezed, then pulled a grubby rag out of his pocket to blow his nose. A small silver coin rolled out onto the floor.

The coachman looked at it, accusation in his eyes. 'Where did that come from, lad?'

'Miss Fairface gave it to me at the stage in

16

London. She said it would start me off . . . she's a kind lady.'

'And what was you a'doing at the stage in Holborn?'

Charlie put his head down. 'Looking for somewhere to go . . . Your Windsor coach had no outside passengers to tell on me . . .'

The coachman grunted, and no more was said while the horses were freed of the harness and led away to be fed and watered, while fresh horses were coupled. Charlie did his bit, proving surprisingly strong and manipulative considering his size and age. Ten or so, the coachman had thought, judging him by the wary, adult gaze. Been at adult work for some time, he assessed. Child and adult all in one.

One of the ostlers who was helping muttered to the coachman: 'An old 'umman came in here and left two parcels for the Castle . . . asked if I could deliver them. Said she wasn't strong enough.'

'And you said "Yes".'

The ostler nodded.

'And she paid you?'

Another nod.

'And you can't do it?'

One more nod.

Not a man to talk much, thought the coachman, but he knew the ostler of old. 'I can get it done.' He held out his hand.

The ostler passed a few coins across to him.

'Is that all?' asked the coachman, still holding out his hand.

After a pause, the ostler passed another coin into his palm.

The coachman nodded. 'That'll do.' He turned

17

towards the boy. 'Carry them up to the Castle gate.'

'They are labelled,' said the ostler.

'Leave them with the guard.'

The coachman sorted out a couple of coins from those he had been given by the ostler.

'Two more when you get back.'

Charlie picked up the parcels, which were long and sausage-shaped and wrapped in sacking. 'Heave,' he said, hoisting one on each shoulder, then staggering slightly.

Slowly Charlie laboured uphill to the gateway with the soldiers on guard. They asked him his business, studied his burden, assessed the weight, and sent him on his way with directions. 'You can do it.'

More slowly now, and ever slower as he went down into the Castle. He thought he was lost, and was preparing to dump his burden and depart, when a pretty woman asked him what he wanted and where he was going.

'Major Mearns . . . bundles to deliver.'

Mindy, for it was she, hammered on the door behind an archway. 'This is it.'

The Major himself opened the door. 'These are for you,' said Mindy. 'Give the boy a coin . . . and a drink; he looks as though he needs it.'

The Major studied the boy and the bundles. 'What's your name, lad?'

'Charlie, Sir.'

'Well, Charlie, where have these packages come from?'

'Left for you, Sir. In the inn below.'

Silently, the Major handed over a coin and a small beaker of beer.

'Thank you, Sir,' said Charlie, drinking gratefully. Then he sped off. He had had enough of those two parcels. Another time, they could walk there, he joked to himself.

He ran down the Castle mound and back to the inn in the High Street. The coach was just departing for the rest of its journey.

Charlie held out his hand for his second payment. 'Did what you asked. Parcels for Major Mearns—he took them from me himself.'

As the coachman paid up, while protesting that it was none of his business and he had been obliging a friend, he said: 'And where will you be tonight?' It was going to be a cold night, and he could not dismiss some feeling for the boy.

Charlie hesitated, then said, 'Miss Fairface said to come to the Theatre; she thought she could find me a place.'

The coachman nodded; this lad would go far. 'And what about your father and mother, do they know you are on the loose?'

'I have no one,' said Charlie.

*   *   *

Miss Alice Fairface might or might not have expected Charlie to come to the Theatre but, when he came, she greeted him with kindness. He reminded her of her young brother, at present on tour in the north of England. Her mother and father were performing in London at Drury Lane. She would like to go back there herself; she was hopeful—she knew she was good. But you needed a bit of luck. Still, you worked where you could and Windsor was a good theatre to which the old King had come. He was mad, of course, but better a mad king than no king at all.

She was sitting in the dressing room where she applied colouring for her cheeks and eyes, and then put on her wig. She had blue colouring around one eye and had been doing the other when Charlie arrived.

'You should have knocked on the door,' she said mildly. 'I could have been in a state of undress. Who told you where to find me?'

Charlie gazed in fascination at her face, one blue eye and one plain. The pink on the cheeks did not quite match either.

'No, no. I came through the door on the side street and listened till I heard your voice . . . You were talking quite loud.' He looked round the room. 'But there is no one here.'

'I was running through my lines.'

She studied his small, sturdy figure. He was not fat, rather thin and under-nourished in fact, but the sturdiness was of the spirit. He was so young—half child, but half old man. What had happened to him in his short life to split him in two?

He was looking at her expectantly, but without trust, as if life had taught him hope, but caution with it.

'Yes, I'm sure I can find a spot. But not for long, you know.' She only had an engagement for a month in this theatre.

'I will move on.'

The door was pushed open. Miss Fairface swung round. 'Oh, hello, Beau.'

Beau was tall, handsome and only half dressed.

'Alice, flower,' he bellowed, 'the costume girl has given me tights to fit a midget.' Beau was his stage

20

name, taken from the celebrated man of fashion, Brummell. Bertie was his real, never-used name.

Hanging over his arm was a pair of white-to-grey tights, meant to be worn with his handsome boots. They did look small.

'Oh, put them on, dear—squeeze yourself in, then go to see her. Or put on a kilt—you wore one when you were Robert the Bruce last week.'

'Good idea, my love . . .' He stopped. 'Who's the boy?'

Alice Fairface hesitated.

'Bring him from London, did you?'

'On the same coach . . . He needs somewhere to sleep.'

'I can pay my share.' Proudly, Charlie produced his handful of coins. 'I earned them carrying two parcels up to the Castle. Precious heavy they were, too.'

'You can sleep back-stage . . . And help with setting up the scene. So, you've been up to the Castle. Did you go in?'

'Up to the gate where the soldiers stand guard and then right up the hill to the room where I had to deliver them.'

'Where do you come from, boy?' enquired Beau.

'London,' said Charlie.

'That's a big city. Won't some person be looking for you?'

Charlie shook his head.

'What about your family?'

'No family.'

He was poorly dressed but not ragged, thin but not starved. A mystery here, thought Beau. On the other hand there were many new orphans. Death

21

came easily and quickly.

'Follow me, lad, and I will show you where you can sleep.'

Charlie bowed to Miss Fairface. 'Thank you, ma'am, for your help.'

'Come and see me again, Charlie. I am here for the next four weeks.'

'I will indeed, ma'am.'

Then he followed Beau.

*   *   *

The parcels were left untouched overnight. Denny and the Major had other things to think about—one of which was a trip to Datchet to see a contact.

Next morning, back in his rooms in the Castle, Major Mearns was unpacking the two parcels. He used scissors to cut the wrapping. As he did so, he began to frown.

'Open the window, Denny,' he instructed.

Denny obliged.

'By God,' said Mearns. 'This is a leg . . . A man's left by the size, weight and look of it. We have been sent a pair of legs.'

'Is it . . . ?' began Denny, then stopped.

'Yes, of course, they're dead,' said Mearns irritably. 'But whether they were cut off when the man was dead or alive I have no means of knowing.'

Denny felt sick. 'You better send them to the Crowners' Unit.'

The Crowners was a newly-formed unit of men, almost all former soldiers, The Crown Keepers of the Peace in Windsor—another sign of the changing times.

Mearns kept quiet. He did not like the Crowners. He particularly disliked Felix Ferguson, a young Scotsman, and the head officer. 'Too cheeky!' was Mearns' comment—'blandness helps you more.' John Farmer he liked a little better, and sometimes took a drink with him. He was a handsome young man. Felix was less handsome, but exuded power—which was what irritated Mearns.

No, in his most honest moments he admitted that he disliked Felix because Mindy liked the man. Also, Felix, unmarried, was showing that he liked Mindy.

Jealousy.

But it was agreed on all sides that the Unit was doing a good job in Windsor. It was small, but efficient. England was changing. Industry was spreading and cities were growing. The Unit was part of that change. Major Mearns felt that he was part of the past.

But he had no intention of going near the Crowners with the legs.

*   *   *

The Unit was at that moment meeting. Felix was laying down the law. His law. He had strong proprietary feelings about the law and Windsor. But what annoyed Mearns was that Felix did not look fierce; he had a quiet, gentle face—almost feminine—with big blue eyes and a crest of fair hair. He had a good army record, though—as Mearns knew—and by all accounts was not one to leave a fight. Otherwise, too confident for anyone's good.

Windsor, with the King in his Castle, was a town that needed the Unit to keep the peace, which, as Mearns admitted, it did well.

It was an efficient unit, and soon there would be units like it all over the country. England was changing. London was growing. Cities were spreading in the Industrial North.

Law and order should be respected. But all the same Mearns had no intention of consulting the Crowners' Unit.

CHAPTER TWO

'Life must go on,' said Major Mearns gloomily. 'Take those legs away. They begin to stink.'

Dead meat, thought Denny. He was a strong meat-eater, but it might be some time before a leg of lamb had much appeal. 'I suppose they are human?'

'Look at the feet.' Only one leg had been unwrapped, but they must match.

Denny had seen many dead feet, but they were usually booted and on the battlefield. The foot he could see now was dirty; it had a large corn on the little toe and broken nails—a foot that had seen a rough, hard life.

'I don't know the foot,' said Denny. Who could? One foot on its own was not easily given a name.

'Take them down to the courtyard and undo the other leg. Then come back and I will join you . . .' He looked into Denny's reluctant face. 'I should smoke a pipe while you do it . . . Come on, Denny—you did enough battle fieldwork.'

Denny grunted as he went out, carrying the pair of legs in the paper of *The Times*. The King would have to do without. The Major considered what he should do. A pair of legs was not a welcome present, and who had sent them?

'And why to me?' he asked himself silently.

He went to the door to shout after Denny. 'See if there is a letter or such in the wrappings. Or if my name is written on the cloth . . .'

'And shall I look to see if there's a love letter inside?' Denny called back with heavy irony.

Mearns lit his pipe, and deliberated on what he was calling 'the matter of the legs'. It was for him to take action. He was the master in this matter. Or so he thought.

The legs could be burnt. Or buried in the Castle grounds somewhere.

He stood up, making himself ready to go out and view the legs. The Magistrate, Sir Robert Porteous, should be informed, and he in turn would tell the coroner, Dr Archibald Devon. The Major knew both men well as he'd had cause to contact them in the past . . . as when the mad servant girl hanged herself and her baby. Except that the baby was not hers—just one she had 'borrowed' for the occasion.

He had found both men humane and reasonable. He did not doubt that good manners would prevail now, but something held him back. They would be interested, so very interested, and he had the feeling that he would prefer this not to be what happened. He was a man for a secret; all his training had reinforced a natural inclination that way.

He would not be breaking any law if he

managed the matter of the legs in his own way. After all, he had the fountain head of all law in the Castle—mad and confined to his own rooms, but still the King and the source of law.

Because of this, the Castle and its environs were a specially protected place—a franchise. The Common Law ran here all right, but its officers, like the Coroner and the Magistrate, were not free to advance in to control what went on, as in an ordinary house.

The Major believed he could act as he thought best, behind this special liberty in the Castle.

'I shall do what I think best,' he said aloud as he walked out of the door. Always in his mind was what William Pitt, then Prime Minister, had said when he sent him to the Castle: 'Remember you are responsible to me, and he who succeeds me. You are there to watch and report. Secret work, Major. As far as the Castle knows, you are there as an old soldier needing a home.'

And there are plenty of them about, Mearns had thought at the time—in the Castle and outside it. The nature of society in the Castle was such that he and Denny were absorbed into the fabric in no time at all, and their presence taken for granted. They were old soldiers living in the Castle.

Mearns was a tall, upright man who still had a thatch of once-red hair—now grey—which he kept well cut by the barber who used to work for the then Prince of Wales. Denny was smaller and slighter, and had lost his hair early on so that his bald head had a fine polish on it. But he and the Major had known each other so long that they matched, making a pair.

The Major was the senior partner and in charge;

26

but Denny was clever—which Mearns admitted.

At the moment, he couldn't see Denny, but he could smell the way he passed. Along the covered way, down a flight of steps into the courtyard, and there he was.

He was sitting on a low stone wall, smoking; at his feet were the two bundles.

'Smelt you,' said Mearns. He was studying the foot. 'That's a working man's foot, not the foot of a gentleman.'

'Somehow I never thought he was a prince.' Denny drew on his pipe.

'He did a lot of walking.'

Their eyes met. 'You thinking what I'm thinking?' Denny spoke first.

The Major nodded. In a level voice, he said: 'A soldier's feet.' He took a pace up and down, then came back to where Denny crouched by his bundles.

'Unwrap the other leg, Denny; I want to study it.'

Reluctantly, Denny parted the sacking, using the knife to cut through the several layers. The smell of dead flesh grew stronger.

'It's stuck,' he complained.

'Dig away!' came the command.

Denny looked around him; he had chosen a spot where not many people came. 'What shall we do if someone comes along and asks us what we are doing?'

'We shall tell the truth—that the legs were delivered as a parcel to me and I am trying to find out whose legs they are.'

'Truth?' thought Denny—ever suspicious of his revered superior. 'I think you know or suspect who walked on these legs.'

The unwrapped leg lay before them, swollen and discoloured by decay. 'That leg was cut off first,' judged the Major. 'It has decomposed more than the other.'

'Or it was kept somewhere warmer,' said Denny.

Mearns ignored this comment; he was staring at a long line of darker blue—almost black—that ran down the muscle of the leg like a seam. It ran in a curve down the leg.

'God save us,' he said under his breath. 'That is a scar.'

Denny covered the leg up. It seemed kinder somehow.

'I know that scar, Denny, and so do you.'

Denny frowned.

'There was blood on it when you first saw it. Blood on all of us.'

Denny looked towards the leg; he stood up from his kneeling position. 'What are you saying, Major?' But he thought he knew.

'A sabre wound. In Spain. You helped bind it up.'

'It's Tommy Traddles.' Denny remembered now; a fierce little fight—part of the main battle. Had they won? He couldn't remember. Afterwards they had been told it was their victory. 'I remember his hurt . . . he was never as careful as we were.' Years ago they had all been young; but Traddles was older than Denny and Mearns.

The Major was remembering too. He turned away.

'Aye. Cover him up again. What we've got of him.'

Just in time, Denny performed this service for

Traddles, as footsteps sounded on the flagstones.

Mindy came across towards them. She looked neat and pretty in her print dress and soft woollen shawl. She had put on a little weight over the years—no longer girlish, but a mature, elegant woman. Usually both men were delighted to see Mindy; she was their friend for whom they felt a warm affection. Which was returned.

Mindy liked and trusted them—which in the society of the Castle was not always the case. She was now an assistant dresser to one of the Princesses, which gave her a security she had not known before. She had one or two suitors, to whom she showed no favours and no preference. Perhaps as a child she had seen too much of the rigours and pains of marriage to be eager for it. Both men thought it would be a pity if she did not marry; she looked born to raise a family and run a neat household. But she must marry well, not for her the destiny of ten children and a basement room. They were looking out for a good husband for her. Denny had thought of her wistfully for years as someone he would love, did love; but he was a humble man and did not rate himself worthy of her.

'So that's where you are. I've been looking for you.'

Denny placed himself in front of the covered-up legs so that she could not see.

But she was quick. 'What are you hiding?'

'Not the crown jewels,' said Denny. 'Nothing you need to worry about.'

The Major said nothing.

Her laugh died away. 'It is a dead . . .' She moved towards the bundles. 'I saw these yesterday

29

when the boy delivered them.'

Mearns spoke up. 'Better not look.'

'It's not an animal, is it?' she said slowly. 'You haven't killed an animal.'

'As soon kill the King,' said Denny with an attempt at lightness. He had no intention of letting her see inside the bundles.

But on the left leg the wrapping, hastily put back by Denny to mask the sight and even more the smell, fell away to reveal the foot.

'Leave it,' said the Major hastily.

Mindy gave a little cry, then put her hand to her mouth.

'Told you not to look.'

Mindy, frozen by the sight, went on looking.

'Mindy,' he admonished. 'You must learn your manners. A lady would not have looked.'

'I'm not a lady.' She had her handkerchief to her nose.

'And before you lose a bit more of your manners, Miss—no, we did not kill him. The legs were a present to me.'

Mindy had gone pale. 'Was he dead when his legs were cut off?'

'I judge, yes.' He hoped he sounded more convinced than he was.

'And they were sent to you? Are you sure they were meant for you?' But she had seen them arrive herself.

'Sent, delivered, given—call it what you like.' He was terse and cross.

'Came yesterday,' volunteered Denny.

'I know that already.'

'We've only just opened them.' Giving them an opportunity to get really ripe, he thought savagely.

30

The trouble with having Mindy as their friend was that she was also their conscience. 'Have you told Sir Robert? Or Dr Devon?'

The Major answered his dear conscience smartly: 'I do not think it is necessary for a member of the Household.' Especially for one who was secretly in the pay of the Cabinet, Whig or Tory, as they came and went. Major Mearns was not a political man himself, and had no vote and no influence; but he recognised power when he saw it.

'Can't be hidden,' said Mindy. She was as conscious of the smell, stench even, of decay as the two men were.

The Major shrugged. 'Who knows?'

'I know. And the person who sent the legs to you knows. And who can tell what other . . .' she hesitated, 'things he may have to send?'

*   *   *

In the Theatre Miss Fairface was shaking out the dress she must wear later as Carmina in *Escape to Spain*, a farce with songs that she was doomed to perform that night as the end of the programme.

'No, Beau, dear, no outing for me today. I must run through my songs . . . written by a man with a tin ear, I vow.'

'The Theatre owner,' said Beau, 'whose slaves we are bound to be while he pays us to perform.'

'You didn't mind playing Falstaff.'

'Oh Falstaff. That was different. That was Shakespeare.'

'Pot belly and all?'

'Belly and all.'

He had been a very good Falstaff—funny, passionate, with a hint of violence, which, after all, is often there in the background with Shakespeare.

Beau Vinter was sitting on a chair in the corner of the room while he trimmed his fingernails. He took up a piece of chamois leather to begin polishing them.

'Yes, Beau, you have very fine nails indeed; but as tonight you play a groom, they might as well look rough and stained.'

'Ah, only "pretend groom", playing at it so I can get close to you, my love, and whisk you off to Spain. It is Spain, isn't it?'

He stopped buffing his nails and went back to cutting one on the right hand which had got badly torn.

He saw Miss Fairface looking. 'It's that fight in the last Act of *Escape* . . .'

Miss Fairface shook her head. 'You take it too seriously, that you do.'

'It's Harry Burgeon, not me. He takes it too seriously, Harry does. Can't act it. I have to fight him off.'

'I wish he took making love to me in Act Three seriously,' complained Miss Fairface. 'I have to do it all myself.'

'Not interested, you see . . . He's interested enough in that lad you brought in, though,' said Beau with a laugh.

'What?' cried the actress with alarm. Broadminded in many ways, as actresses were obliged to be, she was prudish in others.

'Oh, he can look after himself, can that one. He's got a tongue on him . . . "Oh, Mr Burgeon," he said out loud, "you've got one hot hand and one

32

cold. You must have a fever. Shall I call out for the doctor . . . ?" Harry sheared off pretty quick, I can tell you.'

Beau stood up. 'Must be off. I have to check my wig for tonight. Leave it too late and Harry will have my wig and leave me his.'

Miss Fairface went back to brushing her dress, but her thoughts were with Charlie. He was a one, all right. One of a kind.

'Bother,' she said, after a bit. 'Too dark in here for anything.'

She went into the corridor, the better to see how her dress had fared; the light was better by the small window, so she stood there examining her dress carefully.

From there, she saw the boy.

The back of the Theatre opened onto a sidestreet by means of a heavy iron gate. Through the bars of the gate she saw the lad, back towards her, in conversation with a very tall, thin woman; she could see the swirl of the skirt and the edge of her bonnet. Not a fashionable bonnet, so Alice Fairface judged. She stared at the couple for a long minute. It had been a hard year, with widespread poverty, so that there were many children like Charlie on the streets, trying to live.

Then a voice called her and she moved away from the window.

Meanwhile, Charlie laboured up the hill from the Theatre, going slowly because he was carrying a basket that was heavier than he had expected when he accepted the errand. He put down the basket while he stood there, thinking and breathing deeply. Then he turned around, sniffing the air.

Food, hot bread, and sausage and bacon.

He was standing at the head of a small court. The smell of food came from a cook shop in the court. He fingered the coins in his pocket, then made his decision. He picked up the basket and went towards the delicious smells.

The cook shop was dark and warm, with a counter running across the back behind which stood a man wearing an apron, which had once been white but was now blotched with stains of many colours. A small fat woman stood by his side.

Charlie looked around. 'Mulled wine, please, with a hot sausage and bread.'

There was a silence. Then the woman said: 'Are you one of those midgets from the circus?'

'No.' Charlie was indignant.

'Has that basket got an animal in it?'

'No.' He thought this was the right answer; nothing moved in there—that was sure.

The woman considered. She looked at the man and gave a nod. 'Show us your money first,' said the man.

Charlie held out his palm with a few coins in it. Not all he had; he had that much caution.

'Give it 'im,' said the man to the woman.

Silently, the woman pushed a beaker and a plate with a length of dark sausage resting on bread.

'And bread,' said Charlie. 'Fresh bread. Not that stale stuff.'

She obliged, giving him a smirk. 'You're a one, you are.'

Charlie moved away with his plate. From an inner, darker corner came a small figure, even smaller than Charlie, and thinner and older.

A little old man, with grey hair flowing from a

34

skull that was bald at the top, over a face that was wrinkled and shrivelled up into something too old to count. He was wrapped in a cloak, many sizes too big and so old that the stains and dirt of years had settled on it like a shroud.

A whispered croak issued from the lips: 'The wine's all right, but I shouldn't touch the sausage. I think they put dog in it.' A claw-like set of fingers reached out for the sausage. Charlie beat the hand away and started the meal. Then he turned back and handed over half the sausage without a word.

He finished the drink and the bread, picked up the basket and set off again.

He hadn't gone very far before he heard a shuffle behind him, then a bony hand gripped his shoulder. 'Don't hurry away . . . Be careful; they're after you.'

Charlie stopped, letting the basket hang over his arm. 'Who is? Who is after me?'

There was a pause. 'Don't know. Not knowing them, can't say.' Behind the drunken mutter was the hint of a voice that had known education—the ghost of an earlier life. Charlie sensed this without understanding it. One truth he had absorbed in his short journey through the London undergrowth was that what you couldn't understand it was best you moved away from fast.

He did this now, his feet tripping over the cobbles as he prepared to deliver his basket. 'Seems to get heavier every minute,' he said to himself. 'Wonder what it is?' He had a strong, active imagination, so he could call up several pictures.

Books? Heavy enough if you carried enough of them. Boots? Yes, boots and clothes are heavy.

Food? He often thought about food. He could think of worse things to be carrying, but he decided not to. He didn't believe he was being followed, but there was no sense in thinking frightening thoughts and giving yourself a nightmare during the day. He had got enough of those at night: hands grabbing; sticks raining sharp, hard blows on his back; a kick; a slap.

Without meaning to, he put his hand to his ear, as if he felt the slap now.

He looked round, but there was no one there. No one following him. People passing up and down the same path, but not following him. Or even looking at him.

*   *   *

He was observed, however. A sharp pair of eyes was watching Charlie from the window on the top floor of a tall, narrow old house that overlooked the Castle and its hill. 'Oh, I wish I could be there with him—there when the basket is opened,' came the muttered sentence.

Muttered, but audible to the woman sitting on the bed, unpinning her hair. She was not very young, but still comely with pretty, fair hair curving in thick waves. These she fixed with hot tongs, but who was to know?

'Oh, go to . . . You!' she said with irritation. 'I think you only come here to look out of that window.'

They knew each other well, these two; but it was not a continuous relationship. They met as it could be managed.

'Not just that, Dol,' said the man swinging

round. 'Not just that; you too.'

Dol leaned back on the bed with a welcoming smile. She controlled her smile—not too wide. There was nothing personal about this restraint, it was just that she liked to make sure not all her teeth were on show. Some signs of age had to be hidden. Like a gap.

Just between herself and the wall, she wished he'd get all this over with and go; she did have other people in her life.

'Don't take advantage,' she said presently, half languorously, half sharply. 'Not of me.' She knew her way about men. But at times, she lost it.

'What a tongue you've got, Dol. You ought to watch it.'

'Just a little warning.'

*   *   *

Charlie marched up to where the soldiers stood at the guard box—which was what the boy called it to himself. One of the soldiers recognised him.

'You again.' He looked down at the basket. 'For the Major again?'

Charlie nodded.

'Well, take it up. You know the way.'

Charlie had been thinking of leaving the basket here, and then walking away. But now, faced with the soldier, whose face he did not like, it was not so easy. He was not a nervous boy, but he was certainly imaginative.

Little scenes darted in and out of his mind. Now, he seemed to feel the soldier digging his gun into his back to push him on. Or the soldier might open his mouth wide—and wider and wider. Charlie could almost hear the shouts and feel the soldier's hot breath on his own face.

Somehow this steadied him, because he knew that this scene was horrible, but not real; and horrors needed to be real to be truly frightening.

He did not put this into words, but he knew inside him that true horrors were solid and walked around this earth on two feet.

So he picked up the basket and laboured up the path. He certainly did know the way, and if he did not, there was Major Mearns walking towards him, another man with him.

They were not looking at him, but talking quietly to each other. The legs they had been puzzling over had remained unburnt and unburied and were hidden in a wood store outside where they lived; but they could not stay there long . . .

'We could get Mindy to help us. What do you think, Denny? No one knows the inner cellars and caverns of the Castle like she does . . . We could bury the legs and no one would be the wiser . . .

Denny thought about it. 'We would know.'

'You've buried men before, Denny. This is just legs.'

'Then where is the rest of him?'

Charlie spoke: 'Please Sir.'

The Major looked down at him, recognising the boy.

'This is for you, Sir.'

Charlie put the basket down before the Major.

Mearns looked from the basket to Denny. 'You shouldn't have said that, Denny. I think that Traddles is coming home to us in bits.'

Charlie stood there, waiting. Neither of the two men seemed to take in that he was there, or that he had carried the basket up a hill.

He had not been paid very much for his labour. Not enough.

Charlie stood there, legs apart, four square. He held out his hand.

'Please Sir, I want some more.'

CHAPTER THREE

The head stared up at them, eyes open but cloudy.

'I knew it was a head inside that basket,' said Denny. 'Knew it at the first look. Round, heavy, what else could it be?'

A cannon ball, a load of coal, a piece of statuary?

The Major said nothing for a moment while he studied his undesirable and unwanted present. 'Where did the basket come from?'

'From the fishmonger in Market Street. Joliffes . . . He uses such to carry his fish around. He sells them when they get too smelly.' He added gloomily: 'Poor Traddles, dead like that and dished up like a stale fish.'

He looked accusingly at the Major. 'He was a good soldier once. Think of him.'

'I do think of Traddles,' Mearns said. 'But I also think of me. What have I done to deserve this foul honour?'

Into the silence, he said: 'I think it's a case for Tosser.'

Denny looked doubtful. Tosser, as he knew, was drinking more than ever. Not that Denny wondered at this or begrudged him the relief from his life.

'He's buried more than one body. Burnt as well, I daresay, other things too—ways we'd rather not think about,' said the Major grimly, remembering a story about hungry dogs and rats. 'And not on the battlefield like you and me. He can put this one to join 'em.'

One of Tosser's jobs, although not his only one, was to manage the town mortuary—a task he performed silently but efficiently on his own lines; the dead were not allowed to inconvenience him. Rather otherwise—as a stiff arm could support a beaker of ale or a ham sandwich.

Denny shook his head. 'You'd hate to leave even a dead body with Tosser.'

'Which we are not about to do,' Mearns reminded him.

Denny thought that the sad bits of a man that they had were worse. He had liked Traddles—not a good man, but honest in his way.

Tosser, the old villain, lived in one room in a house tucked away not far from the Castle. This room was squalid, but comfortable nonetheless. It made you realise, Denny thought, that the Major was right when he said, 'Never underestimate Tosser; he is cleverer than he looks.'

'Don't bang on his door,' ordered the Major. 'Better to take Tosser by surprise.'

However, they were the ones to be surprised; Tosser was not alone.

A small, shabby figure was crouched by him, holding a beaker to Tosser's lips while drinking from his own. A bottle by his side suggested that he had brought with him what they were drinking. Rum, Mearns thought, by the smell. Both men

40

were well on the way to being drunk.

Tosser was drinking and at the same time stirring a pot on the fire. He was not pleased to see Denny and the Major.

'Not at home,' he said. 'Only stew enough for two.'

'We haven't come to eat.'

Tosser gave a flourish with his wooden spoon so that a strong savoury smell floated out.

'What is it you are cooking?'

Tosser thought for a moment. 'Hare,' he said.

'That smell is never hare,' put in the knowledgeable Denny. One of his army tasks had been to scout for food and then see it cooked. He would cook it himself if necessary. He and the Major knew the value of provender to the foot soldiers. The Cavalry could always eat horse—of which in any battle, victory or defeat, there were always a few dead around.

'Rat, cat and squirrel for flavour,' said Tosser with a rum-inspired giggle.

The Major looked at Denny, then studied the room. There was a bloodstained roll of newspaper in one corner that reminded him unpleasantly of what had come to him that morning.

'I'll cook *you* for flavour if you don't tell me what you are up to,' he said crisply.

Tosser's little friend put down one of the drinks. 'One of the King's pheasants,' he said.

The Major looked sceptical. Not a likely marksman, he thought.

'Not shot, caught. They are tame.' He stood up and introduced himself. 'William Wisher.'

'Willy Wish,' said Tosser. 'Old friend.'

'Mearns,' said the Major, giving Wisher a bow.

'Ah, you got your parcel? I spoke to the young lad who was delivering it,' Willy announced.

'How did you know where it was going?'

'Read it on the parcel: "To Major Mearns". Did it say "with love"? I forget that bit.'

'Do you indeed.'

'Can read. Tosser can't. I can. And write. Latin, French . . .' It sounded like Willy was beginning a list.

'I *can* read and write!' protested Tosser. 'My name. No more indeed.'

The Major ignored Tosser; he wanted to draw more out of Willy. 'Did you see who gave the basket to the boy?'

'No,' said Willy. 'Didn't see. The boy came from the Theatre though.'

'He'll be in trouble there then,' said Tosser with an evil smile. 'One or two down there are partial to lads.'

Willy shook his head. With a chuckle he said: 'He knows how to deal—he knows how to deal!'

There was not much doubt what he meant. The Major turned away; he had his prudish side.

'Tosser . . . Outside if you please.'

Tosser considered, then stood up. 'Willy, watch the stew and don't let nothing burn.' He handed the wooden spoon over to Willy.

Outside the door, he was less amenable with the Major. 'You are getting on, old man; not so young as you were.'

The Major ignored the pleasantry. 'I have something I want you to look after.' Carefully, he handed over to Tosser the basket and a bundle— two bundles, in fact, bound together into one— they were the limbs that had been sent to the

42

Major.

'To bury?' Tosser had performed this service before. Always charging, of course. Nothing came for free in Tosser's world.

Except death. That very often came when you were not expecting it, in Tosser's experience.

'No, not yet; just to keep somewhere chill and quiet.'

'It's dead then.' Tosser spoke with gloomy foreboding. 'What is it then? A baby?'

'Not exactly. No need to go into that. Just keep it safe for now.' The Major turned to leave.

'Not a baby, then,' thought Tosser, meaning to open up the bundle and take a look inside as soon as he was alone with it.

'Don't dig into them, Tosser!' called out Mearns over his shoulder as he left. 'I shall know!'

Tosser was silent—and cross.

'And if you do feel you must look, then wash your hands afterwards.' Mearns warned.

'You're in a mood,' said Tosser. 'In love again, are you?'

'I'm never in love.'

'Saw Mindy with Felix down by the river.' Tosser, no longer able to stay silent, was still cross.

Major Mearns marched off with a straight back.

Tosser summed up the situation. 'He's jealous of Felix and Mindy. Know the signs,' he said to Willy Wish. 'Seen it before. Makes him bad tempered.' He gave Willy a slap on the shoulder. 'Let's eat the stew, then have a look at what Mearns has left us.'

'He won't like it.'

'Shan't tell him. Thinks he can give orders, Mearns does.'

They ate quickly, both of them hungry and both

43

curious to see what the Major had left with them.

'Do you trust him?' Willy Wish had his mouth full, but he got the words out.

Tosser thought about it. Finally he decided, 'Well, you have to.'

'You don't think he's killed someone?'

Tosser thought again. 'He could have.' He knew something of the Major's military career (gossip passed freely inside and then out of the Castle), and guessed what he would do to defend the King. 'He's a soldier.'

'It's his job? But not all the time and everywhere, Tosser.' Willy was earnest. 'Even soldiers can't just kill.'

'He works for the King in his Castle,' said Tosser with the air of one explaining much.

Willy gave a nod. 'Have you ever killed anyone, Tosser?'

Tosser considered what to say. 'Not sure. Might have done. A fight. But I think he got over it. Think I saw him in the market.'

'It was a man?'

'You don't kill women,' Tosser said simply.

'Oh.' Willy considered again. He thought he could have killed a woman if he felt obliged to. 'I think you are a nicer man than I am.'

Silently, the pair went outside to the courtyard where the parcels lay.

'He wanted us to have them,' said Tosser.

'You do look after the dead.'

'Only till they are buried . . . and not in bits. It's been years since we've looked after oddments. And then it was a suicide in the Great Park that the foxes got at.'

'Let's see what we've got.'

44

Silently and with some care, the two men unwrapped the bundles.

The legs came first; by this time the flesh was blue and swollen—decay had set in.

They stared, then passed on. You cannot, after all, identify a dead leg. One of the stray dogs that hung about the mortuary, forever in hope, began to howl.

Without a word between them, they went on to the round object in the basket, which proved not hard to undo.

The face stared back at them, swollen, stained with decomposition, the lips twisted. Willy did not know the features, so he turned to Tosser.

Tosser didn't lose colour or show much emotion, but his expression showed fear. At least, Willy thought it was fear; it might just have been unhappiness.

'It's Traddles,' whispered Tosser. 'My friend Traddles.'

Willy crossed himself in a throwback to the habits of his childhood. 'You know him?'

'Traddles,' repeated Tosser. 'Would you say he was smiling, Willy?'

'No.' Willy had no doubt. 'No, I wouldn't.' It would be worse if he were smiling. It was a death grimace—movement of the mouth as he died. But it was better not to say this to Tosser. He touched Tosser gently on the shoulder. 'Come away, friend. I'll wrap . . .' he hesitated for the right words . . . him? the bits? . . . What should he say? So he said nothing, but pushed away the hopeful dog, and got on with the covering up, leaving Tosser to sit watching.

'The Major will know we looked,' said Tosser

glumly.

'I expect he knew we would.' Willy finished the job—not well, but as well as he could. 'Come inside again now my friend, and have a drink. This has been a shock for you.'

He led Tosser inside.

'You're a good soul, Willy.'

Once inside the stuffy, smelly but warm room, Willy poured some whisky for Tosser, then took some himself. It was his whisky, so he felt able to be generous.

'How well did the Major know Traddles?' he asked.

'Soldiers together. Traddles helped Mearns in his work here in Windsor when he was sober.'

Willy considered. 'So what does the Major do?'

'Don't know,' said Tosser vaguely.

The whisky sharpened Willy's mind. 'I bet you could guess, though.'

'I think he watches all that goes on in the Castle and tells someone back in London . . . Don't know whom, but it would be someone high up. It's an important place, the Castle.'

'Does the Major think it's because of him that Traddles was killed?' asked Willy. 'That, or he killed him himself?'

Another pool of silence.

'The boy who brought the parcels up to the Castle,' Willy went on, 'do you think he knows anything?'

'He knows who gave him the bundles, and what he got for the job.'

'So we could ask?'

'If we could find him.'

Willy thought he might know where to start. 'I

saw him near the Theatre.'

The Theatre was one of Willy's haunts. He knew most of the performers by sight—as they knew him. Even when he could not find the money to buy a ticket, he managed to creep into a seat, and no one turned him out. 'Our Willy', he was called. Not a lot was known about his past. Perhaps he had been an actor himself once and so felt at home in the ambience of a theatre.

'And do you think he'd say?' asked Tosser.

Willy had another of his moments of consideration before he answered. He had in fact more than a flash of jealousy of the lad for establishing himself in the theatre—something which he, Willy Wish, had never accomplished.

'I think he'd tell what he knew,' Willy said at last. 'He seemed an honest lad to me. And bonny. He'd described the woman.'

'It was a woman, was it? You did see then?' Tosser was surprised.

'I was looking that way. Very tall . . . thin . . . hard.' Willy did not miss much.

'You've got good eyesight.'

'I have,' agreed Willy with some complacency. 'Right eye, left eye. I always trust my left eye . . . what it sees is true.'

Tosser did not take up the left eye/right eye problem, about which Willy had spoken before. Often, in fact.

'Be good to find the boy,' he said.

'What's his name?'

Tosser shook his head. 'Might know in the Theatre.'

Willy nodded. 'I might find out there. I am known.'

47

*   *   *

Charlie plodded through the town, down the hill from the Castle, deep in thought. He was angry. He had been made use of.

He walked round the Market Place because he found comfort there. The small shops with their bow-fronted glass windows looked cheerful and prosperous. It was the sort of world he would like to live in, but he knew this was not going to happen. He would be caught and dragged back to London. To the blacking factory—unless he managed to run away again.

He would escape again, of course, and again if necessary. He could not be tethered forever; he knew he was clever. He knew that inside him was a force that could not be beaten. But age came into it; at the moment he was too young to have the use of all his powers.

He hated being a child.

'I've been done,' he said with resentment as he walked on, back to the Theatre. 'I was picked on to carry those bundles to the Castle to give them to the Major. I could go to the clink or be transported.'

Miss Fairface saw him entering the Theatre. 'You look glum.'

'Feel it.'

The actress put her hand in the bag she carried. 'Have a humbug.'

Charlie accepted the sweetmeat which he popped at once into his mouth. Then he smiled. 'Thank you.'

She took one herself. 'So, what's up?' He was

48

silent. 'Or anything more than usual?' she asked with sympathy. She realised that he had had a lot to make him wretched; life was not being kind to him. And she knew how it felt; life often pinched her too.

'Women and children,' she thought, 'we get it worst.' It was sex, really; she would stay with that disability on her shoulders all her life. But Charlie, if he lived that long, would end up triumphant—a successful man. She could see it in his face, hear it in his voice; he knew how to use words. But now something had happened to him which he couldn't work out.

'This isn't just a story,' she thought. 'He's a lad that attracts stories.' She was sensitive to such things; it was what made her a good actress. She knew she had it in her to make a great actress, but life had to offer you the opportunities.

She looked in Charlie's face; in another decade or so, perhaps less, he would be the sort that no woman could resist. And he would certainly have a story to tell—more than one, if she was any judge.

She was surprised that any lad so young could have such a perceptive stare.

'Charlie . . .'

'Yes?'

'Don't you think you should go back to London? To your family?'

'If they want me.' Charlie thought about his father; he might come looking for him, or had perhaps done so already . . . although it was more likely in another week or so. After all, he had only been missing from his workplace two weeks, and who was going to worry about that? Not the man who employed him, and only his father when he wanted to borrow some money off Charlie. 'Always keep some money aside and in your pocket,' his father had said when he got him the job in the blacking factory, not revealing that he wanted the pennies there so he could borrow them.

'Your mother?' He could hear Miss Fairface's voice hinting.

His mother? She would weep when she heard he was lost. She had wept when she said 'Goodbye', yet she had told him how lucky he was and how much he would enjoy himself. No, he concluded on reflection, she would not be looking for him in a hurry.

The actress stared at his face and thought that no boy his age ought to have that look in his eyes. Not that she knew for sure what his age was, and she wondered if he knew; sometimes he seemed ageless.

Then he smiled and the happy boy came back.

Miss Fairface sighed with relief. 'Got a job for you . . . A walk-on in the play tonight.'

'What's a walk-on?'

'No dialogue. You just go on and follow the crowd.'

'Will there be a crowd?'

'Well, not much of one.' It was all being done on the cheap. In fact, Charlie might be the crowd.

'Do I get paid?'

She told him how much, and he nodded as if satisfied. She saw the approval flash in his eyes. 'Just one night,' she said quickly. 'You can't count on the theatre as an earner.'

Depends where you start from, was what Charlie thought. A day walking-on paid better than a week in the blacking factory.

'It's the writer who makes the money,' said the actress. 'A play can go on for years.'

'Like Shakespeare,' said Charlie thoughtfully. The play that night was *Macbeth*. He knew about Shakespeare; his mother used to recite passages, flirting with her big eyes. He had not admired her performance, however.

'You don't have to be Shakespeare.' Miss Fairface thought of all the poor romances and comedies in which she had appeared that had run and run. 'Just give the audience what it wants. You have to find that out, of course, or stumble on it by luck by finding a hole and filling it.'

Charlie thought he would look for that hole. 'How will I know where to go tonight?'

'Follow the stage manager; that's Jack Eden. He's the one with the big nose and the red hair.' Attributes which had prevented Jack from making a success as a performer. One physical drawback you can overcome, but not two.

Charlie had noticed the nose.

He followed the nose later that day, down the corridors, towards the dressing rooms and the stage. Here he was stopped by a harassed-looking woman who told him all that she could allow him for the crowd scene was a cloak. 'Which might be on the big side for you, lad.'

The cloak was black corded silk and velvet. 'Stand up as straight as you can, lad,' said the wardrobe keeper. 'Pity they couldn't get someone taller.' But Charlie dragged the cloak over his shoulders and gave it a kind of a tuck at his neck which shortened it.

He soon discovered that all he had to do was walk behind Miss Fairface. He had the feeling that the stage and performing came naturally to him.

From the front row, the Major and Denny, sitting side by side, had an excellent view. Shakespeare was not the first choice of a play to see for either man, but they had received complimentary tickets from the Manager—a man one did not scorn in Windsor social circles. Also, there was to be some conviviality on stage after the performance that the Major meant to attend.

Denny recognised Charlie and pointed him out to the Major. 'That's the messenger boy.'

'I saw him too,' said Mearns impatiently. He had handed over a few more coins to the lad after the last delivery. You had to admire such cheek. Except it was not cheek, the Major had been around the world enough to recognise the difference. It was a kind of deep self-assurance. 'What's he doing here?'

'Earning. He'll get paid.'

The Major gave a short laugh; he felt sure the boy would get paid. 'He ought to go home . . . if he's got one.'

He watched the performance, deciding glumly that Macbeth had not been much of a soldier and was certainly a poor leader of a country's army. He wouldn't blame it on the man, being a Scot; but Shakespeare he could blame. Clearly the great bard had not understood military matters.

And as for Lady Macbeth—she was such a beauty, mad or otherwise. He could see it was a good part for such as Miss Fairface.

He watched Macbeth advance across the stage to his wife.

'If I'd had him in the army, I'd have made him carry himself better than that,' he thought as he looked. 'Not sure if her ladyship likes his lordship very well either.' Her body seemed to curve away from him rather than cling. But it had been some while since Mearns had had anything to do with a woman (although the Castle always presented offers) and perhaps ways had changed.

The Major's powers of observation had not misled him. Miss Fairface was not happy with her Macbeth.

'You smell,' she whispered, very quietly, her back turned to the audience so that they would not hear. But Charlie with his youthfully acute hearing heard her.

'And I know of whom . . .' he thought.

Beau kept his Macbeth stance, but managed to mutter something under his breath.

'I bet it was that sluttish Dol Worboys,' Miss Fairface hissed back.

'Had nothing to do with Dol for ages.' He pulled away, going into one of his biggest speeches. He had a lovely voice and he did not want to waste a syllable of it.

The audience sat hushed, even as he spun around, treading on Charlie's toe and letting Miss Fairface know that if she made any more trouble he would kill her.

The Theatre was lit by great chandeliers, while wicks in oil held in tin containers lit the stage.

As Beau marched about the stage, proclaiming Macbeth's fate, somehow the bottom of his robe, made of imitation fur, caught Charlie's foot and hobbled the royal progress. He was a good enough actor to build it into his action so that it looked natural, but the glance he gave Charlie suggested that the death threat included him as well as

53

Miss Fairface.

Macbeth is a short play so the party on the stage was soon assembling. There was to be a short interval, with refreshments for those who wanted them, before finishing off the night with a comedy. Charlie abandoned his stage cloak and slid into the crowd.

Major Mearns and Sergeant Denny had also arrived at the party. Across the room they saw Mindy. No surprise there, as the Castle and the Theatre mingled happily. Wine, beer, tea and coffee with cakes and cheese savouries passed between them. Everyone there was laughing as they talked, at least pretending to be happy. In this world, you had to act as though you were successful even if you were not.

Across the room was Mr Pickettwick, who was no more an admirer of the Bard than Denny and Mearns, but liked to be in the social swim. He was talking to the boy, Charlie, beaming broadly and nodding his head, and apparently making a little joke because they were both laughing. He liked the boy—but the boy *was* likeable.

Denny looked at Mearns with a query.

'It's all right, Denny, he doesn't want a boy; he's just a friendly old man. There are a few around.'

'I like the boy myself. He has something . . .' Denny hesitated. 'He's clever; but more than that—you see him looking at the world and telling himself what it means . . .'

'You're confused,' said Mearns kindly.

As they watched, Pickettwick and the boy started to talk to a tall, thin woman who had been standing near them.

'An actress?' asked Denny. 'Don't know her.'

'We don't know them all . . .'

'Had a jolly good try.'

This was true of the Sergeant, although his great protection was that he was never taken seriously—otherwise, as the Major put it, he would have been married off a hundred times since.

The woman was talking away and waving her hands. One had begun to stroke Charlie's head—a hard, strong hand.

Hand still on the boy, she began to promenade round the room, talking to as many as would answer back. Not all did.

Mearns gave a quick laugh. 'Ask her to march.'

'What?'

'Look at her ankles, man, and the way she walks. Women don't use their feet like that.'

He gave another laugh. 'She's a man.'

Slowly, Mearns added, 'and the boy knows it. I think he recognises it.'

'Let's go talk to the man-woman. Bound to be an actor.'

They were walking towards Charlie and the strange-looking figure, who had just been joined by Mindy, when a high scream tore into the air.

The scream came from one of the young actresses—not one whom Mearns knew well, but he thought she was called Henrietta.

Henrietta was standing at the edge of the stage where a passage led into the dressing rooms. She leaned back against the wall, her face white; she was trembling.

'There's a body out there. A dead woman. She's been strangled.'

Mearns left Denny to support Henrietta as he went to look at the body.

'I think it's Dol Worboys,' he said quietly. 'And yes, she's been strangled.

CHAPTER FOUR

'She was always down to be killed,' said Mearns sadly as he looked down on the red, swollen face with its staring eyes. 'Her sort don't often get a quiet ending.'

'No, well, that's true,' Denny admitted. He was leaning against the wall, looking down at the body, one arm still propping up the unlucky finder of it, who was crying gently.

'I always kept my distance, I thought you did too.'

'Her prices were high,' said Mearns. 'But there's more than one way of paying.'

'Eh?'

'Oh, not by me.'

A few minutes later Felix appeared at the off-stage door. He looked at the dead woman. 'Oh dear.' He turned to Mearns: 'You were looking for me, of course.'

'Oh, yes,' lied Mearns, who had been hoping that Felix would not appear. But of course, that was not the way Felix worked. In a theatre or not, he did not like to be off-stage.

The rest of the party were crowding forward to get a look at what had happened. The Major saw Miss Fairface's horrified eyes. She was holding Beau's arm, and the look she gave Beau was enigmatic.

Mearns moved to push them all backwards.

'Don't look . . . Leave it to us.' He turned to Felix who was on his knees by the body. 'We'll have to tell Dr Devon, the Coroner, and Sir Robert Porteous, the Magistrate.'

Without looking towards him, Felix said: 'You forget that it is my Unit that will have to investigate the murder.'

A commanding, stout figure was pushing through the enlarged crowd surrounding the all-too-real scene; some from the audience had leapt across the orchestra pit, or out of the stage boxes, or pushed their way through the side doors. But others were still sitting in their theatre seats, and were beginning to shout for the second part of the performance to start. There was always a lighter ending, often with music and singing, and this was a crowd that wanted its money's worth, real life murder or not.

'Here, here, what is this?' It was the Theatre manager and owner. He got to the front of the crowd. 'My God, what's this?' he said, looking down. 'Is she hurt? Is she dead?'

'She's dead,' said Felix, crisply, standing up. 'Strangled.' He moved forward. 'All this crowd must be moved away.'

It took but a few minutes for those few who wanted to go to leave and the great bulk of those who wanted to stay and see what was going on to be moved into the street, where most stood watching.

'Oh stay, Mearns, dear chap,' the Theatre manager, Mr Thornton, called out as he saw the Major and Denny moving off. Not that they intended to go far. 'And your Sergeant, too.' He knew, as did most people, that when you got the

Major you got Denny too.

'Weren't going,' muttered Denny. 'Just moving my feet.'

Mearns grunted. 'The murderer may well be among those being moved out.'

So the Major and Sergeant Denny remained where they were. As did Miss Fairface, Beau and one or two other cast members. Miss Fairface had edged away from Beau.

'Lucky for you that you were on the stage most of the night so you could not have killed Dol.'

'Don't say things like that,' he hissed back under his breath, a strange light in his eyes.

'But then we don't know when she was strangled, do we? You could have done it before coming on stage.'

'Henry, Henry!' A middle-aged, beautifully dressed woman bustled forward to Thornton.

'What's going on?'

'Oh, my love,' Thornton greeted his wife. 'A death, a murder!'

'Dear me, dear me, that will send profits down and we are on a knife's edge.' Then she brightened: 'But not for long; we shall make it up.'

'Murder,' he reminded her dolefully. 'Murder, my dear. You cannot overlook murder.'

'Who is it?' She started to push her way towards the body. Thornton held her back.

'Don't look, dear.'

She hesitated. 'Someone we know?'

'Only by sight,' he said hastily, nervously.

Rightly suspicious, and knowing her husband, she managed to get through for a look. Then she turned back to him. 'Dol,' she said. 'By sight, eh?' and she shook her head. Mrs Thornton, who always performed in their productions, whether there was a suitable part or not, had cleared her face of make-up and removed her cloak. She had been playing one of the witches.

'Tidy your face,' she said to her husband. He had been another of the witches while fully dressed in his usual trousers and jacket under the witch's robes. Whether this was from absence of mind or for warmth was not clear. These cloaks did service from *Macbeth* to *Othello* to *Mrs Thrufts Heiress*—a very popular comedy in Windsor. So the robes were well known to all the regulars at the Theatre and had caused no surprise to Denny and the Major, who had also recognised Mr Thornton as the First Witch—a good part for him as he never learnt any lines but always made up his own.

Thornton passed his hand over his face, dragging brown powder down onto his collar and making his wife cluck in anger. 'Grubby, grubby . . . no way to meet the dead.'

'She's right about the dirt,' said Denny to Mearns.

'He's probably had that on him since he last played Othello.'

The crowd of onlookers was slowly moving away under the directions of Felix, now assisted by another of his Unit. The chanting from those still penned in their seats, waiting for the performance to go on again, was getting louder. The custom was for a farce to follow the main play and, murder or not, they wanted the farce.

Dol lay where she had fallen, but a sheet had been dropped over the body. Denny drew the Major's attention to a short but elegantly dressed man pushing his way through the crowd. People drew back with respect as he was recognised.

'There's Old Pompey,' said Denny. This was the nickname of Sir Robert Porteous.

Sir Robert, well informed and not a foolish man, bent his head politely towards the Major. He knew that Mearns was, in his way, an important figure in the Castle establishment.

He also knew what many did not—that Sergeant Denny was the Major's ears and eyes in the Castle. He knew that he was sometimes called Old Pompey, and sometimes Old Pompous, and that the origin of these names was from Denny. He was biding his time on that one and would one day get his revenge.

One of the town constables had arrived and he was talking to Felix Ferguson. Relations between the Constables and the Crowners' Unit, as with the Coroner and the Magistrate for that matter, were guarded and cautious.

Felix had been a good soldier—as the Major, who had made enquiries, had to admit—but he had not fought in any battles with the Major and Denny, which made a gap between them. And they judged that, if you hadn't had the touch of the whip from Napoleon, then you didn't know what a fight was.

Denny had been thinking out loud: 'I suppose Dol's death couldn't have anything to do with Traddles? Just wondering.'

The Major did not answer at once; he could see that someone else was arriving. Then he said: 'Possible, but it's a different sort of killing. I don't think Tommy Traddles was strangled; his eyes weren't bulging at all. It looked as if his death had been quick and sharp.'

'Team work, you think?'

Denny had also noticed a new face. 'The Coroner's just come. Thought he wouldn't be slow in getting here.'

The Coroner disliked all the other law keepers in Windsor and, in particular, Felix Ferguson and his Unit. He had no time for the Constable, or for the Magistrate, both of whom he regarded as encroaching on his territory.

'The Coroner's Office,' Denny had heard him proclaim more than once, 'dates back to Norman times when men kept the peace by means of the Frankpledge system.' He would then go on to explain the Frankpledge system—until stopped.

But, like the Magistrate, he too respected the position of the Major and of Sergeant Denny in the Castle. He smiled at them, then bowed. The Major responded in kind.

'Dol will go down to the mortuary once Dr Devon's given the word,' said the Major. 'I wonder how he feels about seeing her this way.' He eyed Denny.

'There's plenty who knew the way to her little cot,' said Denny.

The Major shrugged. 'Who knows?' In fact he did know; he had made it his business to know. Not hard in a town like Windsor to scout around and find out who visited the lovely whore. Traddles had been one of his informants.

'So you think the good doctor will go down to the mortuary with Dol?'

'Sure of it. He'll want to inspect her. Make sure what she really died of, and when. If he can.'

The Sergeant dragged out his own worry. 'I hope Tosser doesn't say anything about our bundles.'

'I don't think he will.'

'It must be getting quite crowded in there.'

'And there's still the rest of Traddles around somewhere waiting to get in,' said Mearns with grim humour.

'I feel a bit nervous, Sir.'

'We've been in worse places, Sergeant.'

'It's not myself I'm worried about . . . It's Mindy. Felix was probably going to walk her home, but now he's bound to stay for a bit and Mindy will have to see herself back to the Castle.' He fixed the Major with his knowing eyes. 'Don't like to think of her doing that.'

Mearns passed over knowingness; it never paid to let Denny feel how clever he was (although in his mind Mearns acknowledged that Denny was exceedingly sharp—which was why he valued working with him). So yes, Denny had noticed how the Major's feelings for Mindy had grown into love.

For that matter, Mearns knew one or two things about Denny that he did not talk about. Denny certainly had a wife in Cripplegate, but he also had one in Winchester, and probably another in Worcester, and another in Widness—all places where his army life had taken him. Mearns wondered if he had always taken care that none of his wives could write so they could not pester him.

But no, that was too devious for Denny. In his own way he played a straight game. And after all, thought Mearns, perhaps they had been glad to lose Denny. He remembered Denny's relief when he met an early romance in Windsor, now a plump commanding school virago.

'Well, Mindy hasn't gone,' said the Major, looking across the stage. 'She's still here. I reckon she wanted to know who was dead. We'll walk her home together and tell her what we know.' Which wasn't much, he thought.

'She'll be safe enough in the Castle,' assured Denny, giving Mearns another knowing look.

'Safe enough from me?' thought Mearns. 'What the hell does the beggar mean?' Denny always meant something by his looks.

'There's one in the Castle who's been seen looking at Mindy.'

'She's a handsome woman,' said Major Mearns.

'Aye, and this is one who knows it.'

'Yes,' thought Mearns, 'me too.'

They were walking towards Mindy, who had seen them coming and was smiling.

'And this one is hard to deny.' This was Denny again.

By now they had caught up with Mindy.

'I don't want to stay,' she told them. 'Let's walk up the hill together, please.' She was always polite.

'I came with Felix but he . . .' she shook her head, 'he can't leave yet.'

The Major nodded. 'I know.'

'Felix sent a message back to me; a poor soul has been strangled. He didn't say more, but all around people were saying it was a woman called Dol. Mr Pickettwick says so.'

'How did he know?'

'The boy Charlie told him.'

'Oh, he'd know all right,' said Denny. 'Can't keep anything from that one. Not anything he wants to know anyway.'

'Denny doesn't like Charlie,' announced

Mearns.

'Oh, I do *like* him; he's a taking lad. But he frightens me . . . he looks through me. Like he could see a joke the other side.'

As Denny had aged, so his voice had got deeper and more uneven; he was a great smoker of a large pipe, which had probably contributed to this. But as well as deepening, so his voice had become gruffer.

'Oh, you're barking,' said Mindy with amusement.

'Like a dog, he can do that!' Mearns smiled.

'A nice little terrier, though, Denny,' said his friend Mindy—ever anxious not to hurt his feelings.

*   *   *

Charlie watched the Major and Denny leave with some wistfulness. He liked Miss Fairface and he enjoyed the atmosphere of the Theatre, but he also felt drawn to the Major and his Sergeant. They were men. He knew this was what he would be one day, but he had not quite got there yet.

Now Charlie had something important to consider: just how safe was it in the Theatre? There had been one murder, perhaps there would be more. He knew it depended on the nature of the killer and his reason for killing.

Charlie had lived and worked in a rough part of London by the river where he had seen violence, and heard of much more, so he was informed about death. He remembered one old fellow he met in the house where he lodged in London saying that there was never just one murder;

64

another always followed, and perhaps another still. 'Remember what I tell you boy,' the old man had said, 'and it may save your life one day.' Even if Charlie did not believe all the old chap had said, and on the whole he did not, he remembered those particular words. So he told himself perhaps he should be wary in the Theatre. And he had another reason for unease: he thought he might know who the killer was.

He stood watching as the Major, Denny and Mindy walked out of sight, and then he turned back to what he was beginning to think might be a dangerous sanctuary.

'I know what I'll do,' Charlie said to himself, 'I'll write it down. Make a story out of it. Then I might show it to someone.'

*   *   *

As Mindy and her escorts approached the Castle, Denny looked up. The first set of windows he saw belonged to Princess Augusta, and next to those were the rooms of Princess Amelia. The two sisters were close in age, unmarried still, and not likely to marry now. The old King, their father, had not encouraged them to think of husbands. They kept themselves old-fashioned in clothes and manner, wearing the hoops and ruffles that the smart ladies of the 'ton' had long since abandoned. They knew they were out of date, but considered that they looked as princesses should.

A few yards further on, and the lights showed behind the silken curtains of His Majesty's suite.

'Wonder how he is,' said the Major, looking up.

'Well, I believe I saw him yesterday,' said Mindy,

'and he bowed at me.'

'Smiled at you too, did he?' barked Denny. 'And blew you a kiss?'

'No,' said Mindy indignantly, 'of course not! He is the King. He just bowed his head. He remembers me from my work with Miss Burney; he was always fond of her.'

At the end of the corridor Princess Amelia appeared. She held a hand out to Mindy. The Princesses too had loved Miss Burney, so that now they had transferred the affection to Mindy. But this had its exacting side, as now she wanted to speak to Mindy and, being a Princess, she wanted a response at once. With a muttered 'goodbye' Mindy went to her.

'And not only Miss Burney did the King like,' thought Denny; a mad king and now a drunken rake for a king. He shook his head. 'But then they were all Germans, not a drop of English blood in them.'

Then he remembered the arrival of the Germans at the Battle of Waterloo, and how well they had fought after their forced march, and the relief it had been to all, including himself and the Major.

'So we were grateful for Blucher,' he conceded to himself. 'Of course Napoleon must have felt less pleased. In fact, if it wasn't for the Germans we might all be French by now!' Denny grinned. 'Not a chance; Napoleon had to go down so we could have our mad king, and our drunk one.'

'What are you grinning at?' demanded the Major.

'Just life, nothing more.' As if that wasn't enough.

'I was thinking about death,' said the Major.

'We've had a bit of that around,' admitted Denny.

'I'd like to get someone inside the Unit,' said Mearns. 'Find out how it works. Check on Felix's progress.' He looked speculatively at Denny. 'You might be able to do it.'

Denny shook his head. 'Not me.'

'Tosser could do it. He'll be helping the Unit anyway on account of holding the dead body.'

'He's got a bit of Traddles that he might see fit to mention,' warned Denny.

'We'll have to do something about that.'

'Like finding the rest of Traddles?'

'Something like that.'

'The best person to get inside the Unit is you,' said Denny, 'no one better, and Felix would take it as a compliment.'

'You think so?'

'Do it the right way; ask it as a favour, and yes.'

It was probably true that Felix wanted to get a foothold inside the Castle—be known as a useful man in Royal circles.

'The big problem for us,' said Mearns, 'is Traddles. Where is the rest of his body? Why are only bits of him being sent to us? Of course, Dol's murder might have nothing to do with Traddles' death, but for now we have to consider that they might be connected. How did she come to be in the playhouse? What did the look mean that Miss Fairface cast on Beau? What is the reason for the killing? And who is behind it?'

'Watch yourself,' said Denny uneasily.

*　　　*　　　*

The light from the Royal window shone down on the two soldiers as they passed by. Inside the Castle, His Majesty—a late riser, day and night seeming alike to him—was being helped into his silken dressing gown, a rumpled bed hung with brocade behind him, while he considered what he should wear for that evening's entertainment with the lady of the moment. Lady Jersey was no longer prime beloved; nor Mrs Fitzherbert. But their memories hung around, like the others . . .

The silk of his gown came from China, its execution was French. Peace with France made such luxuries possible. The silk was blue with deeper blue stripes, with embroidered flowers lurking in the shadows between the stripes. The King's favourite scent of jasmine and rose hung in the bedroom.

His two dressers, both men of some muscle as His Majesty was putting on weight, put a hand under each elbow and helped him to the door, out of the bedroom and into his large, well-lit dressing room, which was also a beautifully appointed sitting room.

While he was the Prince of Wales, and then Prince Regent as his father's health grew worse, he had bought fine furniture—some antiques, some made especially for him. He had exquisite pieces of furniture made by French cabinet makers; he had developed and indulged in a love of Chinoiserie. His suite of rooms in the Castle was so sumptuous, so rich in their decoration (this was only one of his homes) that there had been riots in the streets because of his debts.

And as King, George was no less extravagant.

The dressers helped him to a chair by a small round table, just as another manservant appeared with a tray of coffee. Timing is all-important in Royal circles.

King George leaned back in his chair. 'Those roses are the wrong shade of yellow,' he said petulantly. 'Get them changed. More white in the yellow, and not so much red.' One dresser picked up the bowl of roses and, with a bow, departed. The man who had brought in the coffee poured it from the silver pot into a delicate china cup, then he too bowed and departed. The third stood there until the King waved him away.

The Royal manners were usually good; gentle and polite to everyone, but they lapsed on occasion. Early morning, after a night with too much claret, was a bad time. 'Early morning' with King George often meant, as now, eight o'clock or later in what was the evening for most of his subjects.

His Majesty drank his coffee, then picked up the delicate silver hand bell on his tray.

John, his top dresser, came in bearing a pile of newspapers. The King received them with pleasure. 'Anything interesting, John?'

'Not in the papers, Your Majesty.'

'You are a great news bucket, John, so what is there?'

'A murder in the Theatre tonight . . . You might have been there yourself, Your Majesty. You did say you'd go up.'

The old King George III had been a true admirer of the Theatre in Windsor; he went often and usually insisted on his family accompanying him. The present Majesty tried to keep up the habit; although he was more sophisticated than his father, he still went when there was a particular favourite of his performing.

Miss Fairface was so pretty and beguiling that a visit to see her play, either here or in London, often took place.

'Not when I discovered it was that Scottish play . . . don't care to see a King murdered.'

'And you were very drunk, and Lady Webberly was with you. Drunk also. Her ladyship has departed, if that is of interest to you, Sir.'

'Who was the victim?' He was interested—or half interested at least.

'A woman, Your Majesty.'

'Not Miss Fairface, I trust?'

'No one you would know, Your Majesty. A woman of the town called Dol.'

Into the pause, the King spoke sadly: 'Doll Tearsheet, perhaps?'

'I don't think so, Sir.' John was puzzled.

The King rose and walked to the window; he drew back the heavy silk which covered the pane. Through the glass he could see that the Great Park lay bathed in moonlight. 'Get me some claret, John.'

John bowed and departed, shaking his head. Outside in the antechamber, he met the other two dressers.

'Is it the black jacket or the deep red to lay out?' asked one, a pair of dark narrow trousers hanging over one arm. The King's former love of rich brocades and silks had been changed by Beau Brummell into a quieter elegance.

John shrugged. 'Leave it.'

'How is he then?'

'Bad,' said John, 'very bad. He asked for news and I told him about Dol's killing. He didn't like what he heard.'

'But did he know her?'

'I don't think he knew her; he has the pick from the top of the pile—which poor Dol wasn't, as we all know—but I think any drawing near of death disturbs him.'

He knew, as did the other men, although it was never to be touched on, that this King had inherited more than a crown from his father.

*   *   *

I have been—between ourselves—very ill indeed, the King had written to the Countess of Elgin, *and it is little known how ill I have been*. He gave her no details.

He had to pretend, to act a lie, even when he felt mortally ill; for had not the Duke of Cumberland spread a lie that he was mad?

Mad?

But, of course, it was known.

At Court people knew or guessed. It was inevitable that the word should spread around at Windsor, from the highest to the low. But it was risky to whisper the word 'madness'.

'Keep a still tongue in your head about it,' John warned his fellow dressers. 'For I swear I think he will kill anyone who speaks out of turn.'

Or have them killed.

CHAPTER FIVE

That evening, over several glasses of mulled burgundy (by courtesy of the unknowing but generous King), it was decided that the Major should go down the hill to the Unit, making some excuse which he could surely think up, and have a good look round.

He knew where the Unit was housed; he had made earlier enquiries and it had not been difficult getting the address. Gracious Street, which lay towards the little town of Egham, was not one of the more prosperous or grander streets of Windsor; but nowhere in this Royal town was really poor, so the small houses of Gracious Street were well cared for.

The Unit rented a room at Number Seven.

'Do you know the landlady's name?' asked Denny.

'I do. She's Mrs Brewer,' answered the Major.

'Brewer is it?' said Denny. 'She were Brown once,' he said reminiscently, 'besides various other names.'

'Like that, is it?'

Denny shrugged. 'I daresay she might have known Dol. Not saying for sure because I don't know for sure. But that's all in the past. Or I daresay it is,' he finished, hedging his bets. 'Now she's got Felix in the house it would be better if so,' he ended.

'You're a well of interesting knowledge, Sergeant, or should I say sink? I must remember that.' But he spoke amiably; he had known for years the sort Denny was—indeed, what he was had made him more useful.

'Perhaps I should send you down to Gracious Street after all!'

Denny grinned. 'I haven't seen her for years, and she didn't live in Gracious Street when I knew her.'

'Don't go on.'

'I think they knocked down where she did live, turned it into a hospital.'

'I'll get down there in the morning,' Mearns said. 'Do you know how they are getting on?'

Denny did. 'Felix has three helpers, all old soldiers, including John Farmer, who might be useful. Brewer would like them; she always had a turn for soldiers. They go out and walk the town while he stays inside, unless one of them comes back with a tale to bring him out. But sometimes he just goes out—when they're not expecting it, like.'

'To check up.'

Denny nodded. 'It's what I'd do. You too, I daresay.'

Thoughtfully, the Major said: 'I'll go to Gracious Street first. Early. Talk to Felix if he's there and then take a walk round the town myself.'

'I could do that part for you,' Denny offered.

'No, you stay here. In case another bit or two of Traddles turns up.'

'Wonder if Mindy's been down there for a look?'

'It wouldn't interest her.'

'No, you're quite right . . . that's not what interests her.'

The Major bit back the retort that came to mind, while resisting the temptation to give Denny

73

a sharp kick. Instead he said: 'So I'll be off early tomorrow. Shall I give your love to Mrs Brewer?'

'She'd never remember me, Major. And you don't think I let her know my real name?'

'As long as you use it to me, Denny.' He looked into his glass. 'Another glass of burgundy, please. I don't think His Majesty would grudge us it.'

'No, he's a generous man,' said Denny, his speech slurring slowly. 'A gentleman.'

The definition of what made a gentleman, indeed the very idea, had been changing slowly over the last few decades. Certainly not a knight in armour; more a man who had a feeling of respect towards those lower in the social scale. The Major's view on what made a gentleman was one who looked after his men, and cared for them in the battle—and after it—as well as he could. And who would see that their wounds, lodgings and victuals were taken care of before his own.

After all, they did this for their horses, so why not their men?

Judged this way, some officers were gentlemen and some were not. The Major remembered that the great Duke himself, although he thought his army was scum, nevertheless got the badge of a gentleman.

'Not that we ever thought of it like that, or said so; but we knew it. "He's a good 'un," we said,' thought the Major.

'You've gone quiet,' said Denny, as he poured the Royal burgundy.

The Major said slowly: 'You know the King has not. The King is not quiet.' He drained his glass. 'Let's have another drink.'

They finished the bottle.

74

The Major awoke late, his head aching (the burgundy could not have been as good as he had thought). But after a breakfast of hot tea and a slice or two of ham, cut thick, he felt better. Denny did not appear, but there were signs that he had breakfasted and gone.

Major Mearns walked slowly down the widening path, out of the Castle and into the town. It was a fine morning, although chill. He was not an admirer of natural beauty; too many rough campaigns had made him sure that all he demanded of the scene was that it should be quiet, warm and dry.

Outside the gate was a small figure, standing there silent and still, as if on sentry duty.

'Charlie.'

The boy did not answer for a moment, but stared, eyes quiet and interested.

'What are you doing, boy?'

'Just looking, Sir.'

'For anything?'

No answer.

'For anyone?'

Charlie gave a smile of great sweetness. 'No one to talk to in the Theatre.' Suddenly his face had a pinched look.

'Have you had anything to eat?'

'Theatre people don't get up,' said Charlie regretfully. 'Don't eat breakfast.'

'Follow me,' said the Major, leading him down the hill to the coffee house in the side alley.

'Hot coffee for me—the strongest and the

hottest,' he ordered. He gave the boy a questioning look, and continued the order to the proprietor: 'Same for the lad and some hot bread for him.' Then he turned to look at Charlie again, and added, 'make it two, he's hungry. Had nothing to eat.'

'He'll say a prayer for you,' said the proprietor, giving Charlie a steady look, which the boy returned with the look of one who has learnt how to live in the world and to accept breakfast when offered, even if one has eaten much already.

As the Major was drinking his coffee while considering what to do next, a tall, thickset fellow swaggered into the eating house and sat down in the corner near the fire, where he was promptly served with cooked ham and toasted hot bread.

Before he was finished he was given a beaker of ale and, stretching out his hand without a word, was given a small glass of something infinitely stronger. At no time did he utter a complete sentence.

He stood up to go, still not uttering a word. He took a few puffs at an old black pipe, which was then thrust back into his pocket—still alight as far as Mearns could see. Then he was off.

'A quick meal,' remarked the Major.

'And a cheap one,' said the proprietor grimly.

'Does he come every day?' asked Mearns, who had observed that no money had passed hands.

'Not every day—just when he can.'

'But you are always ready for him?' The ham and toasted bread, the ale and the whisky, had all been to hand.

'It pays.'

'Who is he?' But he was already making a guess,

76

and asking himself: 'Why didn't Denny and I think of this?' But of course, in a way they had and did the same, but it was the King they took from, rather than some other patron at a coffee house.

'Jim Fox—he's one of the Crowners' Unit . . . You know what that is?'

'I do.'

'He's off to see Felix, another fox,' said the proprietor, who seemed a man of literature. 'Last night's killing made them jerk. Poor Dol . . . Did you know her, too?'

'I knew who she was.'

The proprietor's face accurately reflected his view that everyone said that.

Mearns stood up, fastening his jacket. He felt invulnerable when he had that coat on, tightly buttoned. It had seen him through Waterloo, a battle in which he had not actually fought, but in which he had been getting ready to do so when Blucher had arrived and Napoleon had yielded. 'I'm off.'

Charlie swallowed his mouthful. 'Can I come too, Sir?'

Mearns strode away without answering, but Charlie followed. No one had asked him, but he had learnt lately that a cheerful smile together with a polite voice opened doors. And he was curious, very curious.

Deep inside him, so deep it was almost unconscious, was the feeling that events had a shape, and if you followed the first event then you would see the shape. The story.

He followed Mearns' broad back down the hill into a part of the town he did not know. Nice enough little houses, though; he had seen enough of the back streets of London to know what made a slum.

The Major strode on and Charlie had to step out to keep up with him.

He wondered what sort of story he was making up inside himself now. Well, a woman had been killed; that was a start. He frowned; he thought he'd like a bit of laughter somewhere in any story that was his, and it didn't feel as though there was much of that in this killing.

Looking ahead, to his surprise, he saw Mr Pickettwick apparently coming out of one of the houses down the road. Pickettwick advanced towards the Major, holding out his hand in greeting.

The Major responded by taking his hand with a good shake. Charlie could only see the Major's back, so he could not see if he was smiling, but he guessed he was. Mr Pickettwick was smiling, anyway.

'He's a good smiler,' Charlie thought; they were genuine smiles. He was beginning to assess smiles, although what Mr Pickettwick's smile meant this morning, he was not sure.

It really wasn't a morning to smile, in his opinion—not after a murder.

Once they were talking, Charlie kept his face down, staring into the gutter, until the two men began to walk on together—almost as if they had met by plan.

He went on watching them with interest, his mind busy arranging them into his story. In his tale, the two men had met to call at a house down this road.

Mr Pickettwick broke off his conversation on

the murder of Dol, the whore of Windsor.

'Is the boy with you?'

Mearns did not answer for a moment. If he had said anything straight away, it would have been 'Yes' or 'No'.

'He is following us,' observed Mr Pickettwick.

'He could be,' agreed Mearns. He took an unobtrusive look. 'Take no notice. Ignore him.'

'Seems like a nice boy, speaks well, some education . . . He ought to go home.'

'If he has one.'

'Where's he living?'

'In the Theatre, I think. It can only be temporary. Are you staying in Gracious Street, Mr Pickettwick?'

Pickettwick gave his sweet smile. 'No. I have been visiting a friend in Ellen Street.'

The Major mentally assessed the inhabitants of Ellen Street. He kept a kind of an address book in his head. The Barret family in the first house. Miss Macaulay in the second; a highly respectable lady, she had taught in the schoolroom of the younger Princesses. Even he did not know who owned or lived in the next house, which had recently been sold. The last house in the row was the dwelling place of Amy Delauney, and he certainly knew who she was: the beautiful, elegant, more-expensive equivalent of poor dead Dol. Not a bad house visit if you fancied it. She was lovely and willing—very willing the gossip said—but she was also willing to use a little blackmail if necessary. Some thought it worth it, as she was not unreasonable. It depended on how you felt about that sort of thing. 'Miss Macaulay,' went on Mr Pickettwick, 'a friend of my daughter.' The Major remained silent with his thoughts.

'Ten minutes with her and then how long with her near neighbour of the lustrous hair and friendly nature?' thought the cynical Major. 'Wonder how the two women get on?'

'I'm on my way back into town,' Pickettwick explained. 'No more news about the sad killing last night? No, I thought not. You would have said.'

'Don't you believe it,' thought the Major, 'I keep my own counsel.'

'I have promised Mr Thornton a drink of some good Madeira this morning . . . he will tell me what he knows.' Mr Pickettwick held out his hand.

The Major shook it. 'Take the boy with you.' Mearns turned his head to look behind him.

The boy had disappeared.

*   *   *

There was no difficulty in finding out which was the house from which the Crowners' Unit managed its affairs, because Felix's head was visible through the window. He had his back to the window, talking to a man inside, but he turned around, still talking. Then he saw Mearns.

The Major gave a wave as he advanced up the garden path. They had never worked together. He knew what Felix was and did, just as Felix knew, within limitations, what Mearns did, but that did not make them friends.

Mearns was jealous of Felix—plain, straightforward, manly jealousy on account of Mindy, and he could see that Mindy liked Felix. He did not try to stop being jealous. Jealousy was not a wine to drink in moderation. Better to get drunk on it and get over it.

*   *   *

The front door was not locked—hardly practical to have it locked with members of the Unit coming and going all the time. Felix advanced to meet Mearns while beckoning to the other man to whom he had been talking, nodding him to the way out. A big burly figure, he brushed against the Major, but touched his forelock politely as he did so.

Addressing Felix, Major Mearns said: 'Just calling to see you.'

'I wondered when you'd do just that.' He led Mearns through to the room the Unit used, and spread out his hands, as if offering a display. 'You see us as we are—a bare room. Don't be mistaken though.' He tapped his forehead. 'It's all here.'

'Best place for it.'

'Same place you use, from what I've heard.' It was true enough that Mearns wrote very little down, even delivering important reports by mouth. He had learnt that much of politics: trust no one.

'Everyone says you are doing a very good job. That's what I hear.'

Felix nodded. 'Good. You want to talk about poor Dol's death? That's it, isn't it?'

'I don't deny it.'

Felix walked across the room to a cupboard in the wall, from which he took a bottle and two glasses. 'Let me offer you a drink.' He poured a good measure. 'I was advised to keep a bottle of brandy in case I should need to receive a lady in distress or a gentleman suffering an injury.'

'And have you?' The bottle was half empty.

81

Felix gave his charming grin. 'Not so far. But I have several times felt a little strained myself.'

The Major looked at his glass, studying the colour and smell. 'Rum,' he said aloud.

'I fancy it works better than brandy, and I prefer it myself.'

'What more is known about the death of poor Dol? Is her killer known? Or even caught?'

'Not caught, of course,' said Felix soberly. 'Not known either.' He paused, then went on: 'She was strangled . . . you saw that for yourself. Strangled by a pair of hands.'

'By a man then?' the Major suggested.

'It does seem likely, doesn't it? One of her . . . customers—an unsatisfied one?' There was a note of doubt in Felix's voice. 'But the poor young actress who found her . . .'

'Henrietta Temple,' prompted the Major, thinking it was the first time anyone had called Henrietta 'poor'. 'Young', yes, but not 'poor', as she specialised in rich protectors—one of whom was a Royal duke.

There was a hint of a smile at the back of Felix's eyes, which suggested he knew all about Henrietta.

'Yes, she says she saw a woman disappearing into the darkness. Dressed all in black.'

'So the strangler could have been a woman?' The Major wanted to follow this through.

Felix shrugged. 'No one else saw a strange woman in the Theatre that night. Doesn't mean anything, of course. The play was *Macbeth* after all; there were a lot of people going round dressed in dark cloaks.'

'The three witches, for instance?'

'The Thorntons—husband and wife—were two

82

of them,' said Felix, with that smile again.

'They were all on stage for most of the performance. I could see them lurking around,' said the Major reluctantly. He did not like Mr Thornton and would have been glad to have had him for murder. 'Perhaps his wife pretended to be both of them . . . she's large enough.'

'Whoever it was, it scared that poor young woman who saw her,' said Felix sardonically.

'Ought to have had some of your brandy or rum ready for the poor girl.' Mearns was enjoying his own potion, while wondering why Felix was being so generous.

'She was given some water. Women are tough, you know. And an actress . . . trained to recover quickly.'

Their glasses were refilled, then Felix said, with some hesitation: 'There has been some trouble in the Theatre lately . . . I have been looking into it.'

'Ah!' thought Mearns, 'so that is why I got a welcome. He wants to tell me, and find out what, if anything, I know.'

'Thefts?'

'No, I don't believe that would disturb them so much. No.' Again some hesitation before stating: 'Blood . . .'

'Nasty.' It was all Mearns could say as he gulped down some rum. He was thankful Denny was not with him, because for sure Denny would have claimed the blood for Traddles. He could almost hear Denny's voice: 'That's Traddles' blood . . . so that is where he was killed and cut up.'

His own voice was echoing it, but silently. Yet he knew he had to say something.

'How much blood?' he asked at last—his voice

steady, trying not to sound too interested.

'Two or three pools in the yard behind the Theatre. It leads on to Waterloo Place.'

'Then on to Peascod Street.'

'That's right.'

'You can see why the blood and now the killing are making them all nervous.' Felix was walking slowly round the room as he spoke.

'You too,' the Major thought to himself. 'You need help, my friend. This is too much for you, Felix, and you don't know what to do.' He decided to tell him.

'Someone will know who killed her and someone else will know about the blood.'

'Do you think so?'

'Yes, you just have to keep asking. It's how it works.' The Major tried to sound decisive.

'God help me,' Major Mearns thought, 'I hope I'm right. Always worked inside the Castle, but that's a special world. No secrets inside the Castle. In the end someone always tells you.'

'Where is her body now?' he asked.

'Down the mortuary,' replied Felix matter-of-factly, adding: 'The Coroner's orders.'

The same place Traddles was. Or parts of him. The dead calling to the dead.

*   *   *

Down the road, Charlie had crawled out from behind the holly hedge where he had hidden after realising Mr Pickettwick was talking to the Major about him. He had nothing against Mr P—a nice, jolly old fellow who knew where to keep his hands, which was not true of all. In any case, it had not

84

taken Charlie long in London to learn how to deal with gropers and graspers. His first friend, Gog, had instructed him: 'You are a pretty boy, Charlie, and round here you can use that for money, if you choose; but don't go free. Teeth, nails and feet, Charlie; use 'em. You can practise on me.' Which was good of Gog, but Charlie had not done so. There was one lesson he had already learnt: never trust anyone.

He emerged from his hiding place in time to see the Major go into a house further down the road. Whose house it was he did not know, nor why Mearns should be calling there, but in the story he was forming in his head it was because there was someone living inside with whom he must speak.

Yes, that was it, an important interview was about to take place. But there his plot stopped for the time being. Real makers of plots, he told himself, waited to see how the story grew. He would have liked to have a scene of jokes and laughter here, but nothing would come. He had already discovered that such scenes were hard, but joyous, to create. He walked down the road just in time to see Felix come out to greet the Major. Then they went into the house.

Charlie would like to have followed. He could see the two men talking together. He liked the Major better than Felix; he seemed the stronger and the kinder of the two. It would not do to rely on any man's kindness, of course, nor did he. But if he had any trust in his heart, then he felt it for Mearns. For Denny, too—he felt he could make a friend of Denny. It was his secret wish to have a friend.

A narrow, muddy passage ran between this

house and the one next door. Charlie took himself down the passage, half crouching and stumbling in the mud.

There was a side window through which he could see the two men inside, talking and drinking. He nodded and thought that that was what men did. He himself had once been offered an ale and some stronger stuff, but he had had one taste and not enjoyed it; nor had he felt confidence in the motives of the man who had offered it. One swig and he had felt woozy—a feeling half agreeable and half alarming. In the world in which he moved, it was best to keep on your own two feet, with your eyes wide open.

As his eyes were now.

He had got round to the back of the house where there was a patch of sad-looking grass and a small shed in which a cat had taken up residence. The cat looked sleek and well fed.

There were two windows for him to look in. One was large and uncurtained, allowing him a good view of a totally empty room. Bare boards on the floor, no furniture, but a wall cupboard into which, to his annoy-ance, he could not see.

The next window was small, high up, and uncurtained like the other one.

He moved on to look in to the smaller window. By reaching up, hanging on to the slate windowsill and dragging himself up, Charlie could see into the room.

This room was bare of furniture, but it was not empty.

On the boards a thin figure was lying on a pile of rags, and covered with a stained old blanket. Older than Charlie, taller and thinner.

By the side of the lad, pressing against his side, was a starved-looking terrier.

The dog looked up at Charlie. Then he moved away from the boy towards the window. Charlie saw he was lame; he limped on his left back leg.

'You don't look like a biter,' Charlie said.

He dragged himself on to the sill, pushed open the window from the bottom, and squeezed through. The air in the room was frigid, as if it had stored up the cold.

The dog gave a soft growl and the boy on the floor rolled over and opened his eyes. He reached out his hand and the dog came close. They huddled together.

'All right,' said Charlie. 'Friend.' He knew fear when he saw it.

The boy thought about it. 'Spike,' he said at last.

'And the dog?'

'Dog.'

So no name there, just 'Dog'.

'What do you do?'

He thought again. 'Sweep,' he said.

Charlie looked around the room. In one corner stood a big broom. And it was true that, although empty, there was no dust in the room.

He turned back to the boy. He had got used to the signs of starvation and ill treatment in London. He had learned to recognise them, and he saw them here.

'Are you hungry?'

Spike nodded.

Charlie had in his pocket two large sausages that he had bought the day before against his own hunger during the day. What meat had gone into the sausages he did not know, but he expected them to be tasty enough.

He produced one, which he handed over to Spike. Then he saw the dog's eyes following it. 'You're hungry too?' He handed the other sausage to the dog, who took it gently and neatly, taking himself off to one side of the room to eat it. Spike nodded and smiled.

'A nice pair,' thought Charlie. 'I am on your side.'

He went to the door, which was not locked, and opened it on to a narrow passage. He stood listening.

Voices. One he knew was the Major's, and the other was that of Felix. Charlie crept down the corridor to listen. The first word he heard clearly was 'blood'.

. . . it cannot be blood from Dol; she did not bleed,' said Felix.

'Might be an animal's blood . . . cat, rat, dog.' This was the Major.

Charlie at once thought of Dog. Dog limped. But no, no sign of blood. So not Dog's blood, nor Spike's.

'Pity we cannot say whose blood,' said the Major.

'No way to do that.'

'No.' To Charlie's sensitive ear it was not clear if the Major was relieved or disappointed about this. 'What will you do about the blood? Can't leave it there.'

Felix was dismissive. 'I have someone who will clear it away . . . sweep it into the drain.'

'Spike!' thought Charlie.

Charlie went back to Spike. 'Listen, I am your friend. I will come again. Trust me.'

He patted the lame dog and crawled out of the window.

Coming down the lane, he met the Major walking through the gate.

They walked up the road together, side by side, not speaking.

CHAPTER SIX

Eventually, when they got to the hill that led to the Castle, the Major said: 'So what were you doing down the hill?'

Charlie was silent.

'You were following me?

'So I was,' the boy said after a pause. 'I wanted to see where you went.' He considered telling Mearns about Spike and the dog, but decided to wait. He liked the Major, but life had taught him to be cautious about confiding in anyone.

'You saw where I went. Any good to you?'

'Yes,' said Charlie. 'I wanted to know where Felix lived.'

'He works from there. Can't say where he lives.' In fact, he did know; he made it his business to know that sort of thing. So he could have told the boy that Felix lived—perhaps with a woman, but no wife or family—near the river, by what had been the town of Windsor before William the Norman and his son built the Castle. They had even built the hill on which it stood, making the unfortunate English labour and dig to make the hill.

'The English got the better of William in the

end,' thought the Major. 'Not many years ago, the descendants of the Norman lords were calling themselves Englishmen. And speaking English.'

'You still look a bit hungry,' said Mearns, giving the boy a searching look.

'I am hungry.' Charlie was already regretting his sausages.

The Major made up his mind. 'Come up to the Castle with me, lad, and I'll see you get something. I could do with a meal myself. We eat when we feel like it, Denny and I.' He gave his generous smile. 'I don't know what we have in our larder, but I can go down into the kitchens where I will be given something. They are easy there and eat well, so we shall get something good: cold meat, a grouse or a chicken—something of that sort.'

'Won't the King mind?' asked Charlie, running to keep up with the Major's long strides.

'His Majesty? Generosity itself. Besides, he would not know. Much goes on in the Castle that the King knows nothing of, and for certain all he wants from the kitchens is excellent food—which he has got by hiring a famous French chef. But he has no notion of what goes on in his kitchens.'

'Oh, poor old King!' said Charlie with genuine sympathy.

The Major took him straight to the kitchens, where Charlie saw with surprise that there was not just one kitchen but a sequence of them, one after the other.

He said nothing, but his eyes widened.

The Major spoke to a tall, thickset man in a white overall and tall hat. In return he got a bow and a *'Bonjour'*.

'François,' he explained to Charlie. 'A

Frenchman. His Majesty thinks all the best chefs are French. François worked for the Emperor Napoleon.'

Charlie took it all in with an interested gaze. 'The King knows that much about his kitchens then.'

'You are a sharp one, you are,' said the Major, with some admiration. Yes, he knows about the food he eats. Not what I'd want though. Fancy, you know. All looks and no flavour.'

'You've eaten it then?'

Mearns shrugged. 'Only what comes back to the kitchens.'

The boy had left his side to wander between the long tables at which white-coated men were working.

'It's a big meal tonight. Do you call it a "banquet"?'

Mearns pursed his lips. 'I think it is always like this.' He could see that his friend, François, had nodded for a tray to be prepared; he saw the slices of beef go on together with slices of some paler meat, which might be chicken. He was just thinking that something sweet would be welcome when a pie, certainly fruity, was deposited on his tray. 'Enough for six,' he thought, 'but it would never be noticed out of this kitchen. After all, that was what kings were for, wasn't it? Charity to the hungry.'

One of the chefs was talking to Charlie; then Mearns saw that the man leaned forward and took Charlie's arm in a gently caressing way.

The Major frowned. Charlie was an attractive boy. Better get him out of here. Then he saw the boy's heel come down heavily on the chef's foot. Charlie did not apologise—just went on smiling as

91

if nothing had happened.

The Major stopped frowning and gave a small grin. There was no doubt that Charlie knew how to look after himself.

By the time they reached the Major's set of rooms, the tray had arrived and been surveyed by Sergeant Denny with satisfaction. He gave Charlie a nod, but spoke to Mearns.

'They do us well.'

Mearns flicked his eyes towards Charlie. 'I think we owe some of the riches to Charlie here.'

'Oh aye; they'd eat him alive down there, some of 'em.'

'Frenchmen,' said Charlie with decision. 'Any Englishman can beat two of them. Can I have one of those pies?'

The careful Denny held out a plate. 'Just the one.'

While he ate his carefully selected pie, crisp and brown, Charlie looked round the room. It was not large, but it was cosy—a favourite word with Charlie, and a quality he prized. In the middle of the room stood a large, well-polished, dark oak table of some age. A smaller table was in the window recess. Pens and paper indicated it was used by the Major for writing on, although what writing he did was, as yet, a mystery to Charlie. Four dark oak upright chairs to match the centre table stood about the room. One big leather armchair with a matching footstool was near the window, looking out. Charlie instinctively admired it all, but the Major was oblivious, not knowing and not caring that he was using a table at which George I had eaten his breakfast. The Castle was filled with such treasures owing to the magpie hoarders of the Hanoverian House. The more fashionable and delicate mahogany had swept away the solid oak from the Royal suites—but not out of the Castle.

'There was blood in the Theatre. They found it.' Charlie's tongue was loosened by the delicious pie, which gave him a mood of ease and hope.

There was a moment of silence. Denny looked at the Major's face.

'How do you know that?' he asked, speaking for the Major, in whose face he could see knowledge of the blood.

'Yes,' said Mearns, his voice stern. 'How do you know that, my boy?'

Charlie considered; should he tell the two men about Spike and the dog? Caution won. Wait and see what happened, he argued to himself.

'I listened at a window.'

'I don't shout,' declared the Major.

Charlie smiled, then spoke the truth, which was handy for him. 'You're a bit deaf, Sir . . .'

He turned towards Sergeant Denny. 'Ask your friend.'

The Major turned to Denny who hung his head and muttered something.

'All right, so it's true,' said the Major to Charlie. 'So you listened and heard about the blood. Yes, some blood has been found. Now forget it and don't say anything to anyone or you will be in trouble.'

Major Mearns had an honest heartiness about him that made you believe him. 'He matches his furniture somehow,' Charlie thought, 'and both are in good order.'

The Major stood up. 'I'm going to the Theatre.

93

If you have finished eating, come with me.'

Charlie wanted both to go with him and to continue his conversation. He did so as they walked together.

'But the dead lady was strangled . . . no blood,' said Charlie. He had managed to get a look at her, and had been able to observe this much at least.

The Major thought it best not to answer this, so he went on in silence. Charlie continued for him.

'Those parcels that I carried up to you . . . I was paid . . . but they were heavy.'

'So they were,' agreed the Major.

'And the second one smelt.'

'Did it now?'

'I remember thinking that it was a leg of lamb that had hung around too long and had gone a bit high.'

The boy was gazing hard into the Major's face. 'So what were they?'

'Don't you think about it, lad. Leave it to me.'

'They weren't really pieces of meat, were they? Not from an animal, anyway.'

Mearns gave Charlie a sharp look.

'Were they human legs?'

The Major did not answer.

'Why were they sent to you?' asked Charlie quietly.

This was a question the Major had been asking himself, and now he thought: 'Perhaps whoever sent it thought I ought to know. Wanted me to know.' But the Major did not say this aloud.

'And the other bundle, the one that was round and heavy . . .' Charlie could guess what was round and heavy. He lost a little colour.

'Forget it, boy.' He was only a boy, thought the

94

Major. 'This is all rubbish.'

But Charlie was thinking, a deep frown creasing his forehead. 'Am I right? Are they bits of a body? Where's the rest of it? Is it on the way? Where is it now? Where the blood is? Is that what you're going to the Theatre for?' Charlie thought of Miss Fairface. What would she say? A body in her Theatre. Because it *was* 'her Theatre'. While she was performing in it, no one else counted. Mr Thornton—or whatever he was called—did not exist.

Charlie prodded Major Mearns further. 'Is that what the woman who was strangled saw? Did she see something?'

'I have no idea,' said the Major. 'Or not much of one. Dol knew something. Whether she had seen anything or not is another matter.'

'She might have seen the killing. Or she might have known where the rest of the body is.'

'We can leave that to Felix,' said the Major, trying to end the boy's line of questioning.

But Charlie read in the Major's face that he intended to sniff around. 'You need a dog for that,' he thought, 'and I know one. You need a keen sniffer who wants to find food. The lean, hungry and nameless dog with Spike was such a one. But I shan't tell you that; it's my secret.'

The two of them walked to the Theatre side by side. They passed through the front of the Theatre, which was being brushed out, although to Charlie's young nose there was still that smell of cheap wine, ale and tobacco smoke, not to mention body odours—smells that were less pleasant.

The Major passed through without comment; old soldiers had smelt everything.

Charlie cast an assessing eye over the rows of narrow, wooden seats that faced the stage. He had stood at the back last night on one of his wanderings round the Theatre.

'Don't look comfortable,' he said.

'Not meant to be comfortable.' The Major strode on. 'Keep you awake—that's the idea. Drink too much and get comfortable, and you're off.'

'I wouldn't go to sleep; it's exciting.' Just how exciting the Theatre, plays and the performers were, Charlie was beginning to realise. He wanted to be part of it.

The Major turned and looked into the boy's face with a sympathetic smile. 'No, I don't think you would do,' he said. Then he marched on, through the backstage area to where the woman had been killed.

The Major had protected the boy from a good sight of the dead woman; but Charlie had seen a strangled woman near the blacking factory, so he knew what she would have looked like.

A swollen, flushed face with the eyes popping out, the lips drawn back over the teeth in a smile that was not a smile—he had indeed caught a glimpse of Dol's face.

'You'd better get back to see Miss Fairface—see if you can do any errands for her. She may want something.'

'And you want me out of the way because you are going to look for the blood in the yard,' thought Charlie.

*　　　*　　　*

They both saw the stain. The blood had been

cleared away with sawdust thrown over the area, but the deep redness showed through like a shadow. It looked like a map of the world.

'Traddles' blood,' thought the Major to himself as he took in the scene. 'Must be. So he was killed here, poor bugger. Who was he after then? He must have been accusing someone of something. He never did have much sense. Spoke out of turn. Thought he was safe here with all the theatre people around. Unless it was one of the theatre people.'

He looked up from the bloody stains to see Miss Fairface come out of the Theatre.

'Look after your own doublet and trews,' she was saying over her shoulder.

'Only a press with a hot iron—a wash, if you can manage it.' It was Beau following her.

He had a pair of silky black pantaloons over one arm. 'It's for *Hamlet* tonight.'

'I'm an actress, a performer—and a better one than you are, my friend, so don't ask me to do your washing.'

She looked towards Charlie and smiled.

'She likes me,' he thought. 'That was a real smile.' He was learning more about himself and how others saw him with every day in this town. But soon he would have to go home, but which home? Certainly not the blacking factory. But he knew he would have to meet his parents because without that meeting the wound in him would not heal, nor life go on. And life was his job; he would laugh about it, write about it, invent it. He could feel it bubbling up inside him.

The Major had a stick with him, which was not only strong and thick, but pointed. He walked around the bloodstain, poking.

It did not go in.

'Nothing buried here,' Charlie decided.

'It's all solid stone there,' volunteered Miss Fairface, who was also watching.

'The dead woman didn't bleed,' put in Beau, who was, Charlie decided, always going to be someone who stated the obvious.

'This blood came from someone else,' said the Major. 'Or some animal.'

'Mice or rats. Plenty of both round here.'

Mearns looked around. 'No bones.'

'The cats round here are hungry,' said Miss Fairface.

She was a hard woman, Charlie decided; nice, but hard . . . Perhaps actresses had to be like that. It was something he might aim at himself.

Outside the yard was an area of rough grass where a carter kept his old horse. The Major looked towards it, then walked out. Charlie followed him and did the same, but at a distance.

'Your stick is going in more easily there, Sir,' he said to the Major who had begun to prod the grass. 'Ground must be softer.'

'Aye,' said Mearns. 'Or dug over.'

'A hole, Sir?'

'Likely, likely.'

He looked around for something to dig with.

'There's a spade behind the stage,' volunteered Charlie. He was a sharp observer of the world around him. 'It's not very big, but it might do. I don't know what they use it for.'

'It's a prop,' said Miss Fairface, 'for a play about Adam and Eve; it was used in the Garden of Eden.' She saw their faces. 'It's all right, it was a comedy. You didn't have to believe it.'

'Nor do you have to believe her,' put in Beau. 'It goes with a bucket of sand in case we have a conflagration.'

Charlie looked at him with intensity, fascinated that someone really used words like that which he would only have used as a joke.

'Go and bring me the spade,' ordered the Major, giving Charlie a nod. When he came back with it, Mearns said: 'You can dig.'

Charlie thought for a minute, then held out his hand. 'How much?'

'I'll see what the job's worth when you've done it.'

Charlie grinned and got down to it. He was a good bargainer.

He shovelled away; the earth was soft and damp. After a bit, he raised his head.

'I'm getting there.'

The Major turned towards Miss Fairface and Beau. 'You two still here?'

They didn't answer.

Charlie stopped digging and looked down into the hole from which a smell began to rise. Then he quietly said to the Major: 'I can see a dog's head.'

Miss Fairface gave a little scream. But she did not move away. No scream from Beau; already he seemed to have melted away.

'If you're going to stay, then keep quiet,' ordered the Major.

Mearns came up to where Charlie was digging. He bent over the hole, then straightened himself: 'It's Traddles' dog,' he said briefly. 'The rest of it is there, buried.'

'Sure?' asked Charlie.

'I recognise it. He loved it. The only thing he loved.'

'At least it got buried,' Charlie thought, 'not like Traddles,' realising that whoever had owned the dead dog was also likely to have owned the body parts he had carried.

'Shovel the earth back, cover him up,' ordered the Major.

Charlie bent to his job.

'What sort of dog was he?'

'Just a tyke Traddles picked up from the gutter as a puppy, but it was a decent dog.'

But Miss Fairface—with the sharp eyes of the performer (actresses, she had once said, have to see everything: which man will protect them, and which will seduce them and run; and is that a real diamond or paste?)—had seen something.

'Stop! Underneath the dog—I can see clothes. No, perhaps not clothes, but red stuff . . . silk maybe.'

'Red silk?' Charlie looked. Yes! There was a hint, a flash of redness beneath the shaggy fur.

The Major pushed him aside to look. 'Yes, I see something red. But silk? How can you tell?'

'I can't of course,' she said, 'I'm just guessing.'

Using his stick, the Major gently moved the dog's head to get a better look at the red. Delicately, he dragged at the cloth, catching a glimpse of what was beneath. A small piece of the material stuck to his stick as he drew it out.

'It *is* silk. And red—or was once. Stained now.'

The torn triangle that the Major had on the end of his stick was marked with brown. He put it back in the hole. 'Cover it up,' he ordered Charlie.

'If you say so.'

'I do.'

Charlie finished up his work, then held out his hand. The Major was not ungenerous.

'Come to my dressing room,' Miss Fairface said to Charlie as she left.

'Put the spade back where you found it first,' the Major ordered, as he also departed.

Charlie nodded. As he took it back, he found himself wondering what thoughts had crossed the Major's mind as he plucked out the stained red silk.

Whatever those thoughts had been, he decided, they had not been welcome ones.

*   *   *

Sergeant Denny was asleep in the big leather chair by the window as Mearns came in.

'Yes, my darling,' muttered Denny.

The Major pinched his arm. 'Who are you calling "darling"?'

Denny opened his eyes slowly. 'Well, not you.'

'I hope not.'

'I was dreaming,' said Denny with dignity. He got up.

'There is some tea in the pot, and porter on the table.'

Mearns drank the tea thirstily, then moved on to the porter. He drained the beaker and set it down with a bang that announced it was now business.

'So, what have you done today? What is new in the world?'

'Nothing from London,' Denny said carefully.

'So, what else?'

'His Majesty rose late, as usual. Lady Hertford

wanted to see him.'

Lady Hertford had been the object of an obsessive love (although she was said to grant him no favours) for many years. She was not classically beautiful, but she had a handsome, well-developed figure which always attracted the Prince Regent—as he was when their liaison started. Lady Hertford was the woman for whom he had cast aside Mrs Fitzherbert.

'I thought she was dismissed.'

Denny shrugged. 'So did the King, he hid in his bedchamber until she was gone. Then Lady Coningham arrived.'

'The "Vice Queen", as they call her.'

Denny nodded. 'So His Majesty came out . . . Only Lady Hertford had not quite left so the two ladies met.'

'Only wanted the Princess of Wales to come,' said Mearns.

'They got better than that; Queen Caroline appeared with two of the Princesses, Amelia and the little one whose name I always forget. She had dragooned her sisters-in-law (for they do not like her) to come with her. Of course, they hate the Vice Queen even more, even the little one.'

'Sophia, that would be.' The one that is as quiet as a mouse. The old King, their father, George III, would not let them leave their mother, or get married. 'He has a lot to answer for,' the Major always thought. A couple of the girls had escaped to make suitable princely German marriages, which were not much to the satisfaction of the present King, who was busy turning himself, as far as he was able, into the civilised English gentleman. 'So what happened?'

'That's all I know,' admitted Denny with regret. 'The Mistress of the Robes and one of the King's Gentlemen swept everyone into an inner room.'

'It'll be all over the Castle tomorrow—today even—so we shall know soon.' And a finely embroidered version it would be, as the Major well knew, but none the worse for that. Denny was only one amongst many in the Castle for enhancing a piece of gossip and sending it on its way.

Sergeant Denny nodded at the prediction, then sat looking at the Major, waiting. He knew this man; there was more to come.

'I visited Felix today.'

'I know,' said Denny. 'Then you came back here with that boy.'

'I talked with him—not a man after my own heart, but clever.'

'So will he keep the peace in Windsor?'

'He is the sort of man who will be used more and more in policing in the town. All towns; London will get its share. He talked, but not much information was passed on to me. He knows more than he is telling.'

'Not like you then,' thought the cynical Denny.

'But he told me about the blood at the back of the Theatre.'

Denny nodded.

'I thought it my duty to investigate the blood. I went to see it for myself.'

'I'd have come too if you'd asked me. Find anything?'

'We found a hole; my stick sank in the soft soil. So Charlie dug it up.'

'Did he now,' thought Denny. He stood up. 'Come on, out with it! I can see there was something—you've been so long-winded about it.'

'I thought I might find the rest of Traddles' body.'

'And did you?'

'No, just his dog.'

'Foxy.' Denny looked sad.

Mearns nodded. Denny could read his face. 'And something else?'

'Yes. Underneath, wrapped in silk, was a baby.'

*   *   *

Charlie had not wasted his time with Miss Fairface. He had eaten well with the Major and Sergeant Denny but, mindful that he did not know where his next meal would come from, he hid food—a good thick wedge of it—from her tray in his pocket. Thanking Miss Fairface, who was about to take a short rest before her performance, Charlie left the Theatre. He was more convinced every day that he liked Theatre people, but was unsure if he himself wished to act.

He passed up the road, then down towards where Felix had his office.

Mr Pickettwick, taking the air, saw him. 'Where is that boy going?' he asked himself out loud. Pickettwick was planning to visit his London home to check that his business was being well run. Although he often claimed that he was retired, and devoting himself to his literary and historical interests, this was not strictly true; he still kept a keen eye and a strong hand on his affairs. Meanwhile, his 'literary and historical pursuits' were assumed by the cynical but uncensorious Major Mearns to be various young men in the

Royal Guard—or any of the young actresses and pretty ladies who caught his eye. Pickettwick was a man of broad tastes. The equally tolerant Denny judged that there was 'no harm in the old 'un'.

The unknowing Charlie passed on to a point where he could watch Felix's quarters without being too noticeable himself. The house seemed quiet, so he moved closer, still listening and watching.

Then he slid round to the back of the house, to the window through which he had previously seen Spike and Dog. He saw Spike at once, with Dog close behind him, as if they could never be parted, which Charlie reckoned was pretty near the case. They had each other and that was all.

'Well, you've got me now, too,' Charlie thought conclusively.

'Spike?' said Charlie, uttering the name softly.

The lad heard his name and looked up, but said nothing. The dog looked up too, his eyes sharp. He gave his tail one quick flick.

'He knows me,' Charlie thought with satisfaction. 'Knows I'm a good supplier!'

Spike had a wet mop in his hand. It looked as though he was cleaning the back yard. Possibly the house too. He was slave labour.

'You've been working?'

Spike nodded, words not being his medium.

This was when Charlie noticed a long length of thin rope tied around Spike's ankle with the other end attached to the big, heavy door.

'Not so clever,' he thought. 'I can untie that.' He looked into Spike's face and wanted to say: 'Untie—then I tie you up again—and your slave master will never know you have been free. You can escape!'

Then he thought: 'But this is your only home and shelter. Here you have a bed and food, even if not much. If you leave here where will you go? Only to the streets—and I know what that is like!'

So he handed over the food from Miss Fairface's tray, half to Spike and half to the dog, then left.

'I'll be back!' he said aloud. 'Let me put my thinking cap on.'

He looked up at the other window. The room with the cupboard—what could be in it?

*   *   *

While he was talking to Spike, the Major was talking to Sergeant Denny: 'I want you to go to Tosser, ask him to come and meet us at the Theatre yard.'

Tosser, the mortuary man—yes, Denny saw the point of that.

'Then go to the coffin makers in Bell Yard and get two baby's coffins.'

CHAPTER SEVEN

'Two coffins?' Denny queried, although he had done what was required and had hefted the two tiny boxes over from Bell Yard. God knows they were light enough, and would not be that much heavier when filled. 'Two coffins, and here they are.'

Bones of a baby and a dead dog.

The Major read Denny's face. 'The dog

deserves a decent burial too.'

'I had to pay him.'

'You'll get your money.' The Major had the money ready in his pocket, ready to hand over as soon as he saw the two small caskets.

And there they were on the grass before him. The old horse came over to see what they were.

'He takes his money seriously, does Bell Yard Billy.' The Sergeant and Billy met occasionally over a drink in the Duchess of Hanover's Arms, but they were not friends.

'He does—in fact it's said he lets his coffins out to rent. A rented coffin. After the service and before the burial, the body is tipped out and covered in earth and you take the coffin back, for further use.'

'He won't be doing that again,' said Denny with some satisfaction. 'He has a broken nose and a black eye. Seems one parent recognised a coffin he'd bought and paid for being used again . . . more than once. So he went in, gave Billy a black eye, and got his money back.'

The grey had finished investigating the two coffins, then turned away.

'Small enough?' asked Denny.

'Even smaller would have done.'

'Yes.' Denny felt the pinch of pity himself. Strange really, he and the Major had buried bodies enough after a battle and felt nothing. Perhaps you needed the fighting to harden you.

Nor did he look forward to the job to be done. He had buried many bodies, but never dug one up before. He took the lid off one coffin to take out a small hand shovel and a pair of gloves; from both a faintly unpleasant smell floated.

The Major looked at them.

'I got them from Tosser . . . he said I'd find them useful. Uses them himself on occasion, when the need arises.'

'It will very soon,' said Mearns.

Under Mearns' direction, Denny began to clear the earth away. Soon he stopped digging and turned towards the Major. 'I've got there.' He put on the heavy gloves, and with their help eased the dog's body onto the shovel. Then with some help from the Major he moved the dog into the coffin. Mearns put back the lid. Some jobs were better closed up quickly. Then slowly, and gently, Denny got the earth off the baby's mortifying body, and got the shovel underneath. The child had been there longer than the dog so the flesh had gone and all that was left was bones. The skull seemed to be grinning at them.

Denny handled the bones very carefully into the coffin in case the skeleton came apart. This done, he gave the Major a nod.

'We'll shoulder the coffins down to the mortuary,' said Mearns.

'Does Tosser know they are coming?'

Mearns did not answer. Tosser didn't know they were coming, but he would soon find out.

From where he had been working, Charlie came up to them with a trolley belonging backstage. He had guessed it might be needed. He pushed the trolley while the two men walked behind. No one said much. Tosser was not welcoming. Never a very jolly chap, as Charlie had noticed, but what could you expect living and working where he did. But he was especially dour today. Charlie, the observer, rather enjoyed the spectacle. 'You never know,' he found himself thinking, 'when a character like Tosser might come in handy.' But there was something about Tosser's face that suggested satisfaction.

Tosser saw Charlie looking. 'Take your eyes off me, young man.'

Charlie did not answer. Then Tosser saw what it was Charlie had on the trolley. He glared at Mearns. 'No room,' said Tosser. 'Full up.'

'Not if I say so.'

The Sergeant moved to stand next to the Major. 'Come on now, Tosser. Just for the odd night or two; we won't leave them here for long.'

'There are times when I hate you two,' said Tosser with feeling.

'We don't always love you, Tosser.'

Tosser was studying the coffins. 'Not very big, are they? So what's in the boxes? Babies? Dwarfs?'

'No reason for you to know.'

'Are you going to bury them?'

'It's usual with coffins,' said the Major evasively.

'Where?' demanded Tosser, who detected the evasion.

'Here, please, Tosser,' said the Major, as if he had just thought of it. 'May move them later. Let's call it just storing them for the time being.'

'It's work for me,' said Tosser.

Charlie realised then that there was a cost to being dead. 'Doesn't cost much though,' he thought as he watched the coins being handed over.

Outside, Tosser had a tiny graveyard. It was overhung with drooping trees, beneath which was a bench. Charlie could tell that it was all much, much older than Tosser.

'What an interesting place,' Charlie thought. In his mind's eye he could see a dark figure sitting on the bench, perhaps dying there. Being found dead. He thought about it for a while, storing it in his memory as something to hold on to. Confidence bounded inside him; whoever was found dead in such a place, it would not be him.

Out of the corner of his eye he saw a large rat strolling across the grass. He was unmoved; he knew about rats, having lived and worked with them in London. This one, though, was a particularly big and bold animal.

'If I'd had a dog with me, I bet we would have found the rest of Traddles' body,' he thought.

A few modest coins were pressed into his hand with the polite request that he take back the trolley.

Charlie nodded. Miss Fairface would not notice if it was there or not, but the stage manager would.

As Charlie walked towards the Theatre he saw Mindy on the path in front. She was too far ahead for him to catch up, which he would have done if he could have managed it, as he was one of her admirers. He thought she liked him too. She disappeared into the side stage door of the Theatre. He wondered whom she was going to meet. He liked a mystery—even a little one.

*   *   *

The Major and Sergeant Denny returned to the Castle. 'I like that boy,' said Denny.

Mearns was not listening. 'We are the only law keepers in this town,' he declared.

'There is the Unit,' said Denny. 'And in the

Castle there are the Officers of the Guard—'

The Major interrupted him. 'We report directly to London.'

This was true and Denny was usually the person who carried the reports to London. But he often wondered if it got far past the polite young man in St James's who took the message in. The days of William Pitt were over.

The Major continued: 'The death of the woman in the Theatre last night may not make a report to London necessary, but I want to find out exactly how and why she died.'

'Well, she was strangled,' said Denny. 'We know that.'

'But why in the Theatre?'

'It may not have been . . . Perhaps she was dragged there, when already dead?'

'And no one noticed? And why drag her there anyway?' said an exasperated Mearns. He shook his head. 'No marks of dragging on her clothes or body.'

'She could have been carried there in a sack or such like,' said Denny, who liked to cling to a point.

'Why? *Why*? For what reason?' said the Major, no less determined—and, he thought, more reasonably. 'No, she walked there and was killed there.'

There was a moment's silence. 'So do I take a report on this to London?' Denny wanted to know.

'No, no. Not yet. There is more to be discovered yet.'

'There certainly is,' said Denny. 'There was more to Traddles than a head, legs and a dead dog!'

111

'And more to be found,' went on Mearns grimly, unconsciously echoing Denny. 'Where is the trunk? The other limbs? Where are they?'

And, 'Where is truth,' he heard himself say aloud.

Denny heard him, but felt he would rather not have done.

'Let's go down to the Golden Crown, get the landlord to give us some of his best and eat some of that ham he keeps on the side. Good stuff.'

'Yes, I'm hungry too.' Hunger and misery felt like the same ache.

*   *   *

Mindy was more down to earth than the Major and Sergeant Denny in her opinion of what was going on at present in Windsor. She was also, in some ways, more observant and understanding of the behaviour of people.

'I notice what's really there, and I'm not sure if the Major always does. Nor Denny. Especially Denny, bless him.'

Women always liked Denny. True, they did not trust him. The sharper of them (amongst which she counted herself) instinctively understood that, trustworthy as they knew him to be as an assistant to Major Mearns, he was less so in his dealings with *them*. He had always treated Mindy with friendly correctness, but she was protected by her position at court and by Major Mearns.

What she had noticed was the eyes of the young actress who had found the strangled body of Dol Worboys. Henrietta Temple was her name—her acting name. The Major had told Mindy that she was really called Hetty Maggins, one of six daughters of a theatrical family. 'Generations of them,' he had said, 'probably one of them cavorting on the stage when Shakespeare was working.'

Hetty—off stage she used that name—was a good actress. She could control her face, and her hands, and she had done so when she came running in, calling out what she had found. But she could not control her eyes and feet. All the time she was telling her tale, she kept looking at her feet, in their pretty slippers; they were never still.

Mindy was one of a crowd hurrying towards the Theatre, but she took no notice of them, not aware that she was observed herself. She was a well-known figure in Windsor, respected and even feared due to her position in the society of the Castle. She had helped as a dresser with Princess Caroline till her death in childbirth, and now she was head of the Castle wardrobe, in charge of the dressers and the sewing maids. More than one hopeful had offered marriage, but Mindy valued her independence with the prospect of a pension and Royal cottage in the Park when she chose to retire. Her experience of marriages was that they were hard work and brought little joy.

She knew the Major liked her, as she liked him, but it needed thinking about.

She hesitated a moment as she came close to the Theatre. Hetty might be angry. She might be angry and frightened after what she had seen. Would that make her dangerous? Mindy shook her head. No, surely not.

* * *

Jack, the stage manager, came out carrying a piece of scenery.

'Is Hetty about? Miss Temple?'

Jack gave her a smile. 'She's in the wardrobe room, sorting out her costume for tomorrow.'

'A good part, is it?' asked Mindy, answering his grin.

'Ophelia, Miss. Miss Temple's best so far.'

She couldn't help asking: 'What about Miss Fairface? Is she in *Hamlet*? Who does she play?'

'Queen Gertrude.' He gave another smile.

'That's a good part—perhaps the best for a woman in the play.' But for the older woman, of course; yes, she understood the smile.

Inside the wardrobe room, Henrietta was studying herself in the looking glass. She spun around when the door opened, a smile on her face. 'There you are.'

'Hetty, can I speak to you?'

The smile faded. 'Oh, it's you.'

Hetty eyed Mindy; she knew Mindy, knew her position in the Castle. 'Yes, but not here.' She looked down at what she was wearing. 'And I must get out of this.'

Charlie, having grabbed a trolley full of clothes with a pile of boots on top on his way in to the Theatre, pushed through the door. He smiled up at both women.

'Busy,' he said cheerfully. 'Plenty to do.'

'Leave the clothes and go.'

'Boots too?' His smile was angelic.

'Of course the bloody boots too.'

Mindy said hastily, 'I'll wait outside. But I do want to talk to you.'

Charlie followed her. 'She tells lies, you know.'

Mindy thought so too, but why did Charlie think it? 'How do you know?'

'I can tell by her face.' He smiled at Mindy. 'I tell lies myself when I have to,' he said casually. 'I know the look.'

'Have you lied to me? Or to the Major? Or to Denny?'

Charlie shook his head silently.

Before Mindy could say anything else, Hetty appeared. She was wearing a neat day dress with a shawl over her head. 'If you want to talk then it must not be outside.' She looked around her. 'In the shed over there.'

This was a wooden box-like structure where stage properties were stored.

'Not locked?' asked Mindy.

'Not locked, we can go in.'

'She's used it before,' thought Mindy. 'Now I wonder what for?'

At the door, Mindy paused. 'There's no need to go any further. I wanted to say that I don't believe you found the body of that unlucky woman. Not by chance. You knew she was there. Perhaps you helped to drag her there?'

Hetty took a deep breath; she rubbed her hands down her skirt before answering.

'That's not true.'

'Oh come on. You're a liar. I'm going to make you tell what you know to Major Mearns.'

Hetty gave her a little push. 'Oh, go in, we can talk.'

Caught off her guard, Mindy stumbled forward, catching her foot on a piece of wood, and then fell. She heard Hetty enter the shed behind her and say,

'Oh, *you're* here!' Then Hetty gave a gasp. The shed grew dark as the door banged shut.

As Mindy lay on the floor with the smell of damp and dirt in her nose, she began to realise that what she had heard had been more than a gasp. She raised herself on one elbow to take in what was before her.

In the gloomy light she could see Hetty lying on her back, with her eyes open.

It was at that moment—when Mindy realised Hetty was dead—that she smelt the smoke, felt the heat and knew the shed was on fire.

She crawled towards the door. By the time she reached it, it was already hot enough to burn her hands.

There were neither bolts nor locks on the door, but someone had pushed a very heavy object against it, blocking it, which she could not move.

She began to shout for help.

'There'll be no one around,' spoke a voice inside her head. 'There never is once the curtain's up. You know that. No one here except whoever did it. Lit the fire and wants you and Hetty to burn. Perhaps they didn't know you were here. Or maybe they just didn't care.'

She hurled herself against the door, shouting. It did not move. Damn! Damn! Damn!

No one came.

She turned in despair to Hetty. No use; she was dead, right enough. There was a bead of blood on her forehead where she had been hit. The blow had dug out a little pit, which had filled with blood.

Mindy shouted again. 'Help! Help!' Then she began to cough as the smoke got to her throat and chest. Her eyes were watering too.

116

She tried to shout again and only a hoarse croak came out. Then she heard a voice.

'Mindy? Can you hear me Mindy? This is Charlie.'

'I hear you,' she croaked as loudly as she could.

'I'm going to get you out.'

'Get help.'

She thought she heard the boy mutter that there was no time to lose.

Then she could hear him at the door. It was shaking and from outside came a rumbling noise. It went on as she listened, and then the door moved.

She stood up, grabbing at the smouldering doorframe. 'I am going to survive,' she told herself, 'I will survive.'

The door shuddered. A bit of smouldering wood, not flaming, but red hot, fell from the lintel onto her face. She could not bite back a scream.

'Coming! Hang on there, Mindy!' called Charlie. Then he shouted: 'Step back! Step back!'

'If I can,' she thought, with the heat and smoke on her back. She wondered if her hair was burning, there was that smell . . .

No, it was Hetty's hair. But she had been wearing a wig, and underneath her own hair was thin and dry.

Then there was a crack of light where a piece of wood fell away from the door and she could see Charlie pushing and pulling—somehow both movements at the same time—at a large box used for stage dressings. As he succeeded in moving the box away, Mindy kicked the door, which opened enough for Charlie to grab at her and drag her through.

'There's Hetty inside still,' she managed to say as she fell into his arms.

He put her gently on the stone flags.

'No, don't go, Charlie. She's dead already.'

'Can't let her burn,' he called over his shoulder.

By this time Mr Thornton had hurried out of the Theatre with his minions by his side. On his instructions they were throwing buckets of water on the shed.

Charlie re-emerged seconds later, dragging Hetty out with him.

'You're a brave boy,' Mr Thornton said to Charlie, patting him on the shoulder. 'Oh my goodness me, that poor woman.' He was looking at Hetty.

She had burned easily. Amazing how the fire had licked over her.

*　　　*　　　*

'You're a brave boy,' said Mindy to Charlie as he helped her back to the Castle. 'I hope the Major does not see us,' she said looking round.

'Why not?'

She touched her hair and thought about the burns on her cheek. 'What do I look like? Tell me honestly.'

'So she likes the Major,' thought Charlie to himself. 'Doesn't want him to see her not looking pretty.'

'You always look pretty, Miss Mindy,' said Charlie with conviction.

But the Major was on the staircase ahead. He advanced towards them, hands held out.

'Come along, my dear. I have been in enough

battles to know that you have been in one.' Sergeant Denny loomed behind him. 'Bring her in—I can help her. Still keep a war chest.' He studied her face as he took Mindy's arm and drew her along with him. 'Those are burns; I know a burn when I see one. Seen worse, seen worse. I can cure those.' He turned to look at Charlie, who was following with the Major. 'What about you, young man, you burnt too?

'Only my hands—a bit.'

'He's a hero,' said Mindy, struggling to speak through singed lips and Denny's soothing touches of some sort of cream. 'Saved my life.'

'Seen a fire before.' Charlie was remembering the blaze in the old stables next to the blacking factory, and the screams of the horses. He had minded the donkey as much if not more than his friend Joe who had worked there. 'Knew I had to be quick.'

Mindy, who could still hardly speak due to Denny's administrations, reached out a hand to him.

The Major was watching Denny at work. 'You're the one to help her, but I think she's had enough of the cream.'

'Needs to stay on as long as possible, that way you'll not get holes and blisters in the skin.'

'You were always good with the wounded, Denny,' remarked the Major.

'Someone had to be.'

'How long have you had that cream in store?'

Denny considered, then said with satisfaction, 'Since Waterloo. Keeps well, doesn't it?'

Mearns knew when he was being laughed at. 'It will be older than you soon!'

119

Denny laughed as he released Mindy. 'Made it for the last ruckus in the Guards' rest room. Had some nasty wounds there.' He smiled, leading Mindy to a chair to rest. 'Who burnt you, my dear? Was it personal or an accident?'

Charlie took a deep breath—he knew what he thought, and what he had seen.

'Tell us,' ordered Mearns. With a few skilful questions he got the story from Mindy.

Charlie kept quiet.

'So you were standing by the open door talking to Henrietta when you either fell or were pushed inside?'

'Pushed,' said Mindy in a firm voice. 'At first, I thought I had tripped, then I thought Hetty had pushed me . . . perhaps she had . . .'

'Then she was pushed in after you and the fire started. An accident?'

Mindy shrugged; how could she know? But she had heard Hetty call out as if in surprise.

'So she knew who was there?'

Mindy nodded. 'I think so.'

'But you did not?'

'I did not see.' She gave a shudder as she remembered how quickly the smell of burning wood and flesh had followed. Whoever had started the fire had not cared whether she burned or not.

The Major turned towards Charlie. 'And you? You were outside; what did you see?'

'Saw a man come up behind Henrietta . . . Mindy was in the shed. I think Henrietta pushed her—not sure about that; I was a way off.' He paused. 'Then the man hit Henrietta, closed the door and set it alight.'

'How?'

'He had a lamp behind the shed, and a brand which he lighted with him . . . held it to the door. He was all ready to do it.'

'You didn't try to stop him . . .'

'The door caught fire at once; he may have put something on it—oil.' You could do that, he knew; he had heard that this was what had been done to the old stables. Word had been that the animals had been smeared too so that they would burn quickly.

The Major saw his face and nodded. 'No, you did the right thing; he'd have knocked you out. Mindy would have burnt like Henrietta.'

'Please!' exhorted Mindy.

'So who was he? Did you see his face?'

Mindy shook her head. 'Didn't see him—only heard Hetty's voice; she knew him.' But she was on her way to being dead.

'What about you lad?'

Charlie shook his head. 'I saw his back, not his face. He was wearing a long black cape with a collar up round his neck and hat pulled low.'

'Oh.' The Major gave Charlie a long, cold, assessing look. Charlie knew what it meant; the Major thought that Charlie might have something to do with the fire. Mindy saw the look and knew what it meant too. She reached out to grip his hand in support. Charlie winced with pain.

Denny noticed the pain. 'Let me get at you, Charlie, and see what I can do.' He took a look. 'You've been in the wars too.' He picked up his pot of ointment, then began to spread it on the boy's hands.

Mearns relaxed. He trusted Denny's judgement. The judgement of others he wasn't so sure about.

'I suppose we shall have Felix and the Unit working on this new death.' Mearns did not rate Felix's powers of investigation very highly. 'And the coroner, Dr Devon,' he added. Nor did Mearns rule out intervention from the magistrate, Sir Robert Porteous.

'It's up to us, Denny,' he said aloud.

*   *   *

In the grander part of the Castle where the King had his chambers, the sovereign was being shaved by one of his valets while a Gentleman-in-Waiting talked to him. At intervals His Majesty took a sip of brandy.

'Go on Wavered, go on! One of the actresses has been killed?'

'Yes, Sir. Looks like murder. Burnt, Sir, burnt to a crisp.' Or so he had been told. 'But she was hit first, then pushed inside the shed and the fire started.'

The King's mouth turned down. He drank a long draught of brandy.

'Does that mean there won't be a performance at the Theatre tonight?' enquired the King petulantly. 'I was looking forward to it.' He added: 'That's the second death there, is it not?'

'The first was not an actress, but a woman of the town.' Lord Wavered stuttered as he spoke.

'You'll fall over your own feet next time you go out, Wavered!' said the irritated monarch. He prepared to let his valet get back to work. 'Shave on. And you, Wavered—get to the Theatre to find their plans.' Then he added, as an afterthought: 'And what they are doing to discover who killed those poor women . . . Not a good thing so near the Castle, not good at all.'

'I'm sure the new Unit will soon find out,' said Wavered. 'And no one would want to harm Your Majesty.'

'You think so, do you? But I have always known you for a fool . . .'

Wavered began to bow himself out. Since the death of the Princess Caroline and her stillborn son he had learnt to be wary of His Majesty's temper. He was in pain too, by the look of him, and far too fat.

The King called after him: 'And if any woman wants to see me, send her away!'

Lord Wavered nodded politely. Any woman indeed—Lady Coningham perhaps? Or the old Queen, his mother. Or one of the Princesses.

He got to the door, bowed again, and fled with relief.

As the valet started with his razor, King George muttered that he had more trust in Major Mearns—*he* was the one.

CHAPTER EIGHT

Mr Pickettwick was the first visitor to the Major and Sergeant Denny that evening, coming eagerly from the town to ask what had gone on, while at the same time anxious for Mindy. 'She was burnt, was she—how? Some say she and Henrietta—such a lovely woman—were locked in on purpose—which is murder, is it not? But Mr Thornton says it was an accident. But all say that Charlie is a hero.'

'He did do well,' agreed the Major.

Mr Pickettwick had come, inconveniently—but he was not a man to know the difference—while the Major and Denny were talking over what had happened. Charlie had gone back to the Theatre.

Or so he said, but the Major wondered. He was beginning to be puzzled by Charlie.

Charlie and Major Mearns were rivals; or rather, that was the Major's thinking. Charlie was not aware of it; that was not how he saw things. He certainly thought about the Major—a fine man. But he had other puzzles, other worries—like the dog and his master. Mearns said to himself: 'There's more to the boy than I saw before. He's brave and clever.'

Major Mearns did not rate himself as clever. Able to deal with situations, yes; but of the two in the team, Sergeant Denny was the clever one. The Major hadn't thought that on first meeting Denny, but over the years he had seen the truth.

'I'd like to find out who killed Traddles,' he had declared to Denny over a glass of His Majesty's wine.

Mindy had taken herself off to rest. She sent a message to the Mistress of the Household, Lady Fraser, to explain she was ill. Actually, she was not, and she told the Major, but she explained she needed to rest. And after all, her hair was singed by the fire and it smelt!

'So would I like to know who did for Traddles. He wouldn't die easily,' said Denny.

'And I think the same person killed the two women.'

Denny was silent while he thought that over, and decided that the Major was probably right. 'I would like to find the rest of his body. Traddles deserves a proper burial.'

'Plenty on the battlefield don't get more than a cover up or left to the foxes.'

'That was no battle.'

'Three dead. Feels like a battle to me,' replied the Major, authoritatively.

'All by the same person? Is that what you think?'

'Yes,' confirmed the Major. 'Let's get who did it. I'm angry!'

It was at this point that Mr Pickettwick arrived.

'Charlie is a very brave boy. All say so!'

'So you told us before.' The Major was friendly, but quiet. He wanted to go on thinking—not gossip with Mr Pickettwick. Mr P, as Mearns and Denny called him, liked a gossip and usually had his packet to offer back.

Mr Pickettwick looked around. 'Is he still here with you?'

'He's gone back to the Theatre.'

'Ah well, he might be needed there. The King himself intends to go.'

*   *   *

The King arrived at the Theatre, dressed in the new style of black suiting, beautifully tailored and with a white shirt. He had left behind him the gaudy silks and velvets of his youth, admiring the style of Beau Brummell—which he now tried to emulate. He stroked his arm in an unconscious preening movement.

Mr Thornton came forward as he approached. 'Your Majesty, Sire!' He was bowing low and walking backwards at the same time while holding

125

two candelabra.

'Yes, yes, Mr Thornton!' snapped the King. He liked people to remember he was the King and to treat him with respect, but Mr Thornton always overdid it. 'Pray, be careful, Mr Thornton, you will fall over again.'

Thornton stumbled at that moment. A backward trip was difficult to control with his serious gout, and it looked for one moment as if he might grab the monarch's arm to right himself. Just in time, Lord Eaden, the Lord-in-Waiting, stepped forward and saved him from falling.

'To my box, Sir!' announced the King, with irritation. 'To my seat, if you please.'

When the King was seated in the box, he patted the seat beside him. 'Here for a moment, Mr Thornton; I want to hear about the death of Henrietta.'

The Manager, although flattered to be asked, was also aware that the performance, halfway through, was held up with an irritated cast pacing up and down behind the curtain, while His Majesty was settled in place.

'An accident, Your Majesty, a dire and tragic accident.'

His Majesty inclined his head. A little more information was needed.

Thornton cleared his throat. 'There had been a bonfire of rubbish near the shed; it was thought to be out, but now we think a spark set the shed alight. No one's fault—a terrible happening.'

There was a regal frown. 'But I understand the door was blocked.'

'Oh—not blocked, Your Majesty, just stuck— one of those terrible accidents.'

'Two accidents,' said the sceptical King, who was no fool. 'That's two accidents too many.'

The Manager muttered something about it being the way with things.

'Look into it. Get that man who runs the Unit—Felix or Phoenix, or whatever his name is. He was sent to me to make his bow when he arrived. Or there's Major Mearns—a very good man. You could ask him. Better still, ask both of them.' His Majesty sat back ready to enjoy his evening when the curtain went up. Death was always sad and one did grieve, but there was no point in not taking one's pleasure when it was offered.

Then the tender heart that hid inside his Majesty's fat frame made him remember what a lovely creature Henrietta had been. A tear squeezed out of his eye.

'Get the curtain up, Mr Thornton!' he said loudly. The King took for granted instant action. Royalty does not expect 'No' for an answer.

He settled down to enjoy himself, giving no thought to Charlie, although he had certainly noticed the boy about the place (he observed a good deal, especially people).

Charlie, meanwhile, was on his way to see Spike and Dog. He went into the house his private way: through the back window. No one had tampered with it, but he had been careful to leave it in a position where you would never know it would open and had been opened. He closed it carefully behind him.

The room was empty—no sign of Spike and the dog. He moved quietly out into the short corridor and into the room next door, the room with the cupboard of mystery. There they were, the pair of them, tethered, tied up in rope. True that the dog had been incompetently roped and he had already got a leg out.

'I can soon get you free, Dog dear,' said Charlie, 'and probably you as well, Spike.' He sat back on his heels to consider. Was it wise? 'But do you want me to?'

The boy was silent, then shook his head. 'Only do me up again, tighter, hurt more.'

'That's likely,' said Charlie.

'Free Dog.'

'A pleasure.' Especially as the dog had more or less done the job himself. He knelt down again, this time by the dog, talking to him gently while he undid the knots. The dog gave himself a shake, and was out of the network and free. He trotted over to lie, full length, by the boy.

'Good Dog.'

'I could get you out, too,' offered Charlie again to the boy. 'No trouble.'

The boy shook his head. 'No, I said just get tied up again, tighter.'

Charlie nodded. He knew about the various ways of cruelty. Felix, he thought, excelled in them all.

Charlie had come over to talk to his friend, but could see that now was not a good time. 'I won't forget you,' Charlie promised. He held out his hand to be grasped and the two lads held hands.

'Look after yourself.' Actually, 'don't get killed' was what he meant. There was too much death in Windsor at the moment.

He went back to the Theatre. Flowers and hearts were how he thought of the dead women. Who could want them dead?

He had expected the Theatre to be dark but, no, lights were blazing, noises and music floated out towards him, and Mr Thornton was walking up and down.

'Thought you'd be dark.'

Thornton said: 'What His Majesty wants, His Majesty gets.'

Charlie sniffed the air. He could still smell the fire. Thornton watched him.

'Don't worry, the fire's out.' He added tersely: 'And what was left of Hetty has been taken off to Tosser's. She was a good actress and a popular one, so there will be many at her funeral. Still, she was a worry and a nuisance. Always short of money and drinking and borrowing. It doesn't do, you know.'

'No, I suppose not.' Charlie, who had developed a keen eye for that sort of thing in his London life, saw that the Manager too had had more than a touch of wine.

The Manager moved away awkwardly.

'Oh, watch it, Sir. You might stumble,' exclaimed Charlie.

'You'd make a good writer,' said Thornton, putting out a steadying hand. 'You've got the tongue for it.'

'Oh, thank you, Sir!'

'It ain't a compliment . . .'

'And I know it,' said Charlie to himself. 'But I take it as one.'

'If you ever had to work with writers you'd know what I mean,' Thornton declared with meaning.

'Thanks for telling me.'

'The only set worse is actresses.' By this time the Manager was hobbling off.

129

'But, Sir! You're married to an actress,' Charlie called after him, knowing exactly what he was saying.

He followed the Manager towards the back of the Theatre. 'Like Follow the Leader,' he thought.

As he went towards the dressing rooms, he met Miss Fairface coming out. 'You still here?' she asked.

Charlie nodded. He had nowhere else to go. 'Curtain down? The King gone?'

'He didn't stay long because of the fire and Hetty's death. He thought about it but he decided it wasn't suitable. Also, I think he liked Hetty. Well, we all did—in spite of her funny little ways.'

Charlie looked questioningly at her.

'Well, we all have them, don't we? She liked to tell a tale . . . Might have been what . . .'

Miss Fairface went no further.

Charlie could end the sentence for himself: 'Might have been what killed her.'

'Who knows?' said Miss Fairface. 'But you're a brave boy, Charlie. If it hadn't been for you, Mindy would have died too. But she's got the Major to keep an eye on her. I hope she'll be careful. Whoever killed Hetty might think Mindy knows his name too.'

The conversation had become very grim. 'Think of a joke; think of something funny!' she said urgently to herself. 'You're upsetting the lad, he's gone quite white!'

Charlie did feel a little faint. He wasn't certain who had killed Traddles and Hetty, but he thought he could guess who did know, and he thought he knew why Dol had died. Of course! Tosser knew . . . If he was not the killer himself. Charlie had seen Tosser's face and seen satisfaction there.

*   *   *

It was hard to like Tosser, but even harder to dislike him. There was something hard and solid inside Tosser that meant you had to respect him.

Charlie did not use that word, but he knew the feeling.

Two women were dead. They had the legs of another body, and a head, but the rest of the body was still missing.

'Whoever killed Traddles and Hetty probably killed the other woman,' said Charlie to himself. 'And I want to find out who that person is.'

He made his way to the low, stone-built building which looked as if it had once been a stable. This was where Tosser put the bodies until he was told they could be buried by the Coroner. Tosser did not welcome him, but Charlie had not expected anything better.

'Tosser, those legs . . .'

'What legs?'

'You know—the legs that were found; you have them. What about the rest of the body?'

Tosser did not answer.

'I think you know where the rest of the body is.'

Tosser did not answer but mutely accepted what Charlie said.

'And you know who he is.'

'Just a vagabond.'

Charlie was not going to be dismissed so easily.

'And you know where the bodies go.'

'I did not bury it if that's what you mean, boy.'

'No, I don't suppose you did. But you will know

131

the best burying places in Windsor.'

Tosser did not answer.

Charlie waited, then said to himself, 'I must find that body. I can do it. There are not so many places it could be hidden. Not in the Castle. And Tosser would not put them in his own back yard.'

He must confront Tosser, but he did not look forward to it. He knew where Tosser lived, or thought he did—knew how to find it anyway.

Twice he had followed Tosser home, going as far as he could without being noticed. He had followed a shaggy white dog that had followed Tosser. Follow the dog and he will lead you to Tosser. But as he had hesitated at the top of a short but irregular stretch of stone steps, the dog had disappeared, and so had Tosser.

Charlie went back, deep in thought, to drink some small beer in the drinking and eating place next to the Theatre where they never questioned his age provided he had the coins in his hand.

He plunged straight into some talking. These were not delicate people where you have to lead up to a question or be subtle. He chose the man who had served him his ale, a man who could be talkative and kind. Not clever, but willing to open his mouth, was how Charlie described him.

'Just off Hythe Street, Eton Passage, is it?' That was just the name he had seen on the wall. It did not lead to Eton.

He got a nod.

'Then you walk a bit down the passage, and it's dark, and you come to a row of steps. Where do they go?'

There was a moment of silence when the man he was talking to worked out where he meant.

'Oh, you mean Deader's Steps.'

'Deader's?'

'Bodies, dead people. One after the other, they turn up there. Dogs and cats sometimes . . .'

Charlie stared at him. 'Why?'

'Someone who lives near the steps likes to use them that way. Killed them too, I daresay. Never been copped.'

Another man at the bar leaned across. 'Shut up! You're scaring the boy.'

'Not him.'

Charlie took what was left of his drink to the darkest corner of the room to think about what he had been told.

'I am not brave,' he told himself, 'but there is a story there which I want to know.'

When no one was looking, he slipped away. The walk to Deader's Steps was short. He stood at the top, looking down. They smelt and they were dirty.

Then he heard a dog howling. As he listened he heard shuffling footsteps, stumbling up the steps.

Tosser stood in front of him, his throat cut from ear to ear with blood streaming down and flesh and vessels hanging out. He stared at Charlie, seeing nothing, then he fell forward on his face.

CHAPTER NINE

Mr Pickettwick often said he did not like dogs. Or was it that they did not like him? No, this could not be; dogs liked him because they always sniffed round the edge of his trousers while making little growling sounds.

If anyone didn't like him, it was that tyke Charlie.

Mr Pickettwick found his throat and mouth exceedingly dry; he was thirsty. It did not take long for him to decide to turn into Ralli's, the drinking and eating place—new to Windsor, but very popular because you could buy coffee and a simple meal at any time of the day or night.

Ralli—he liked to be called Mr Ralli as part of becoming English—had been swept up in the train of Napoleon's armies and deposited near Windsor, where he saw the possibilities at once. There was no quarrel between him and Bert Frost who ran the pub a few yards away because both knew that the pub customers would never use Ralli's, and the other way round. It was people from the Castle and rich visitors like Mr Pickettwick who would come to eat and drink at Ralli's.

He bowed when he saw Mr Pickettwick come in. He foresaw profit from Mr Pickettwick.

Or trouble.

One must always be prepared for everything.

*   *   *

Two women and two men all dead. Traddles beheaded, Dol Worboys strangled, Henrietta burnt and Tosser with his throat cut. And then there was the dead baby, too, that the Major had found with the dog's body.

Charlie made the list out in his mind; they were linked, he was sure. For the moment his interest wasn't in who had killed them but in the dead themselves—they should be written about. No need to be too gloomy about it either—not even with the legs.

He had to admit that he could think of one or two good jokes about what those legs could do on their own. Or had already done.

He had lived in the rough part of London, dumped in it by his parents. His mother had been especially keen: 'It's a good thing for you, Charlie; you can earn . . .' With those words she had put a wall between them which he would never knock down.

Yet despite this memory, Charlie had to go back to London; he knew that. It was his place, but he would always be glad he had come to Windsor.

He would be in trouble when he got back to his family; he knew that too. But he would insist on what was right. His rights.

He knew that inside him there was a life bubbling up. He wanted to learn how to develop that energy. It would mean the use of words, because he already enjoyed using them. But he must learn to use them in an educated way.

*   *   *

'The King is mighty fond of women!' Charlie's thoughts were digressing to some words used by Major Mearns. And the monarch was fond of clothes too. Half asleep as he had been that morning, His Majesty had been dressed in blue, red and gold. A kind of gaudy uniform.

Charlie liked clothes, too, but he felt his tastes would run in a quieter way.

In spite of his diversion to matters Royal and what the King liked, Charlie could not stop thinking about the dead souls.

'Cheer up, Charlie,' said Miss Fairface.

'I'm thinking about the dead man.'

'I know.' He might be sad for Traddles, she thought, but he is also very curious. 'And not just a man, Charlie. Two women have died as well, and one was Henrietta.'

'Yes, I hadn't forgotten Henrietta,' Charlie said soberly.

'I'm thirsty. I could do with a drink.'

'Mr Thornton always has something in his room. He'd let you have a drink. I could go and get it.'

'No, Charlie, although it's kind of you. I couldn't drink strong stuff like that—not when I'm working. Mr Thornton wants to put on some sort of performance.'

Charlie pulled his lips down in disapproval.

'No, you can't blame him; it's not his fault. It's either money or the King.'

'The King wouldn't want a performance after what happened.' Charlie was even more shocked.

'Kings can do what they like. Or this one can,' she commented.

A voice called out, 'Miss Fairface, Miss Fairface!'

It was Mindy. She was wearing a trim, high-waisted blue dress with a light blue shawl across her shoulders.

They had known each other for some years, and were friends.

'I've come to see how you are.' She looked at Miss Fairface's downcast face. 'I need hardly ask.'

'I can't help crying. There's been so much death! Am I very red and swollen?'

'Not at all, my dear.'

Actresses knew how to cry without showing the

traces.

'Charlie,' she said, 'go along to Ralli's and bring back some coffee for us all. If you don't want coffee, choose something else. He knows I will pay later.'

'I'll learn to like coffee,' he said to himself as he scurried off. Clearly it was the sort of drink that people like Miss Fairface drank, and he intended to be one such person himself.

'Perhaps I am ready,' the thought came unheralded, but welcomed. He could feel something growing inside him, something to do with Spike and the dog. The dog was important.

He sped off to Ralli's to get the coffee where the sight of Felix Ferguson supping coffee on his own reminded Charlie who was the rat in the woodpile.

Ferguson's gaze flicked over Charlie with cold indifference.

'He saw me though. He knows I'm here,' thought Charlie with triumph, as he waited to be served.

Ralli knew what he wanted. 'Three?' he questioned. 'For you too?'

'Yes,' said Charlie proudly. 'For me too.'

He was carrying the three cups carefully on a small wooden tray when Mr Pickettwick came up beside him and took the tray. 'Let me carry it, my dear.'

He carried it to the Theatre, saying nothing more, until he got there. 'In Miss Fairface's dressing room?'

Mindy and Miss Fairface, who had been talking quietly, looked at him with surprise.

He began handing the coffee round. 'Here you are, ladies. And one for the lad. No, don't say

137

"none for me" as I have had about three cups already. It ought to be champagne.'

'I couldn't drink before a performance,' Miss Fairface declared.

'You ought not to be here tonight, not after hearing the rumours that are going round. Just think, that poor man murdered and cut up just outside,' he said.

Miss Fairface blanched a little. 'Mr Thornton wants a performance here tonight,' she said quietly.

Mr Pickettwick clicked his tongue in disapproval.

'Oh, it's the King really, he wants to see.'

Mr Pickettwick clicked his tongue again and shook his head.

Charlie said: 'Have my coffee, Sir. I have to go on an errand.' He had taken a small sip and decided that, although coffee was certainly a drink to grow into, he wasn't ready to grow yet.

He made his way to where Spike and his dog lived.

*   *   *

It was a small house, one of a row, with two windows on the ground floor, and two upstairs. He went round the back and looked in the first window. The cupboard was open; a woman's dress and shawl were hanging there.

He could see Spike looking at him and the dog beside him. Charlie waved at Spike, and climbed up. 'I'll have to give you a proper name, Dog.'

Dog gave a short sharp bark as if he agreed— even as if he had a name and he knew it; but who else did?

Charlie looked through the window to speak to Spike. 'We'll have to make up a name for your dog. And not just "Dog" either. Give him a bit more, he deserves it!'

The dog wagged his tail. 'Yes, good boy!'

'Good boy,' said Spike. 'Good boy, good boy!'

Charlie studied his face. 'You could talk better than that, Spike, if someone spoke to you. Perhaps you aren't even allowed to talk.'

Suddenly, he found himself asking: 'Is that man Ferguson your father?'

Spike shook his head firmly: 'No.'

'Well, you got that out all right, loud and clear,' Charlie thought. 'He is not your father. Although, goodness knows how you can be so sure.'

He said to the boy: 'I will talk to you, Spike, and to the dog, and you must speak back.'

He looked at the dog. 'Perhaps not you, Dog!'

The dog wagged his tail.

'Now you, Spike. I am Charlie,' and he pointed to himself. 'You're Spike. Say "I am Spike".'

Spike looked thoughtful, then said slowly, pointing at his chest: 'I am Spike.'

'Spike. Spike.'

'Spike,' said the boy slowly and solemnly.

They continued with their conversation through the window—Spike was doing well.

'I wonder if it's that he can't hear properly, as well as no one speaking to him,' Charlie thought.

'Come out,' he called. 'We can't talk properly through the window.'

Spike shook his head. 'Spike can't.'

'He's Ferguson's prisoner,' thought Charlie—he who had always been free.

'Are you hungry, Spike?'

The boy nodded slowly.

'Stay where you are. I will be back. I won't be long.'

As he hurried to the cooked meat and pie shop that he knew, he wondered if Spike would be there when he got back. If Ferguson arrived back, he might send Spike out on an errand.

He ran back with the cold sausage and slices of meat that the shop man had sold him. He was always generous to Charlie, which the boy appreciated while sometimes reflecting that it was not the sort of thing he could have sold at a high price.

'Hungry, are you then?' the man had asked this time.

'No, but it's for someone who doesn't get much. And a dog, too,' he added.

It was then that the bread was put round the meat and another sausage thrown in. 'Thank you, Sir!' said Charlie, looking at the name written above the open-windowed shop. 'Mr Copperfield, Sir.'

'Not my name . . . I just bought it with the shop.'

*   *   *

Charlie handed the bread and beef to Spike, who began to eat, and he threw a sausage to the dog.

'You don't look so thin, Dog,' appraised Charlie. 'I expect you go hunting. A deal of ratties round here.'

He knew he ought to get away, and something of this must have got through to Spike (although not to Dog who was busy eating) because Spike's eyes

140

seemed to say, 'Don't ever leave me.'

'I'll have to,' thought Charlie silently in reply, 'but I'll fix you up with someone before I go.' He climbed down.

'Now finish eating and we will do some more talking . . . I can see you want to and, once you've got the hang of it, then it'll come easy. Talking is natural, you'll see. One day you'll say to yourself: "So that's how it works," and you'll be away.'

Spike opened his mouth as if he was about to speak, then he shut it quickly. His eyes looked frightened and he looked away. The dog moved away.

Charlie turned round to look. There was Felix Ferguson, the Crowner, marching towards him down the alley. Although Ferguson was moving smoothly and quietly, it was a march all the same. He remembered the Major saying that the Crowner had been a soldier. Not a soldier he would care to serve with, was the impression Charlie got.

'I came to have a talk with the boy,' Charlie explained.

'You'd get more talk out of the dog.'

'Spike's got more to say than you know,' Charlie said to himself.

*   *   *

On his way up the hill where the Castle and the Theatre faced each other, Charlie met Major Mearns.

'Hello, boy. Coming to call on me and Denny?'

He was a nice man, which showed in the smile he gave the boy. The truth was that Charlie interested him. He wasn't the usual street boy; he spoke in sentences for one thing, and used words as if he liked them. As a soldier, Mearns was used to observing and assessing, and he found Charlie to be clever. Not sharp clever, nor vicious clever. He'd met plenty of those through the years. But Charlie was a maker—someone who would produce something.

That's if he lived long enough to do it. Living on the street was no recipe for long life. Nor was the army, he reminded himself, so, don't push the boy that way. He ought to go back to his home which, from the look of him, had not been too bad a place.

'Where have you been, Charlie?' Mearns was interested.

Slowly, Charlie said: 'I went to see Spike. You know who Spike is?'

'Yes, I know Spike. And the dog.'

They smiled at each other.

'I like Spike. There's a lot in him,' said Charlie. 'He needs a proper home. I might take him with me when I go.'

'Are you going then?' He wasn't surprised. Who would be? Charlie wouldn't be a boy to stay in a place like this. 'But do you suppose he could cope with your life?'

'But I am easy.'

'But you might create a dangerous world for you both,' thought Mearns, but did not say it aloud.

'I have been thinking I ought to go back to London. I never meant to stay so long in Windsor. But it's full of interesting people like Mr Pickettwick and Denny, and Miss Fairface and the Theatre, and you of course. I suppose I'd be one too, if I stayed around.'

'But not so interesting if you go away to London and make your life there.'

There was a decision in Major Mearns' voice; he had seen a lot of young men grow up (and die), and thought he knew what was best for them.

*   *   *

After leaving Charlie, Mearns went back to his rooms where he found Denny having a drink.

He sat down beside Denny and took a drink himself.

'I like that boy Charlie.'

'So do I. Shall I ask him in for a drink?' said Denny sleepily. This was his usual method of making friends.

'He's only a lad.'

'Lads like a drink, and he's had one already, I'd say.'

The Major did not argue with his judgement. He had known too many soldiers to find it hard to believe. He might even have been a tipsy one himself long decades ago.

'I won't be the one to encourage him; nor will you, Denny.' He held out his own glass, though. 'Fill up, please, Denny. The red wine.'

'The white is better,' said Denny.

Mearns leaned back against the cushions on his chair. 'Do you remember when we had Miss Fanny Burney here as Lady-in-Waiting to the Queen, and we had that trouble?'

'The murder?'

'She dealt with it. I reckon she was cleverer than our Crowner.'

'I always used to bolt my food,' said Denny, 'so I was in time to see her on the afternoon walk with the Queen and the Princesses.'

'I did too,' admitted the Major. 'Only, as I don't eat so much as you it wasn't such a struggle.'

Wistfully Denny said: 'She's a married lady now and lives across on the Continent.'

'She was very clever about the murders we had then. We could do with her now. Our Crowner accepts the bodies, but doesn't do much about finding who put them there.' The Major poured himself more wine. 'I mean to find out.'

'We could start guessing,' said Denny.

'I've been doing that and not getting anywhere.' The Major spoke over his wine, but Denny could tell he was enjoying himself. Also, he thought the Major could probably make a pretty good guess at who was sending the body parts.

'People don't realise what a dangerous place a castle can be,' said Denny. 'Think of the history it's got. It's bound to tell. In the stones.' Denny was a great believer in the past influencing the present.

'Well, don't go and retire on me,' said Mearns with good humour. 'I need you, Denny.'

'I'll stay,' said Denny. 'Couldn't afford to go.'

From the corridor outside they could hear loud voices.

Denny looked alarmed. 'What's that?'

'That's not a quarrel. Don't you recognise His Majesty's voice? All that family talk loudly when they are excited.' The Major added thoughtfully: 'And he sounds more excited than usual. Wonder why?' The Major was pensive. He knew one of the voices: it belonged to Maken, one of the Gentlemen-in-Waiting.

Denny took a furtive glance around the door. He sometimes got the gentlemen-in-waiting confused, but this one was Lord Maken of Muirhead. No one could forget a name like that, especially when allied to rich red hair. And he always had lovely clothes. Rumour had it that he was a 'friend' to Mrs Fitzherbert, and there were some red-haired children in the town.

Behind Maken stood the King. He was wearing one of the beautifully tailored dark cloth suits that Brummell had converted him to. Even Denny admired its stylish, unostentatious elegance. He knew, of course, that it came from the tailor at the end of Bond Street and that, plain as it was, it cost as much as one of the silk jackets that His Majesty had previously admired.

Lord Maken seemed to have visited the same tailor and probably got his silk cravat there too.

Lord Maken said, 'His Majesty would like to speak to Major Mearns, please.'

'Shout at him, you mean. Bellow like a cross lion!' thought Denny. But he knew better than to say anything, because there was His Majesty a little way down the corridor and the Major was in the room behind, acting as if he had heard nothing.

'This was how you behaved at Court,' Denny thought. 'Natural, you were not!'

The Major stood up and bowed. 'Sir.'

His Majesty smiled. 'I want you to kill someone for me.' Mearns allowed himself to look surprised. He had killed enough men in the professional way as a soldier, but once he had retired, he had not killed.

'Is it anyone I know, Sir?'

'My wife.'

Lord Maken made a soft noise like a moan. 'His Majesty is joking.'

Mearns was silent; he did not know what to say. Perhaps if he laughed it would prove it was a joke.

'Yes, poor joke,' said the King, sadly.

'Come back to your rooms, Sir. Let me take you,' said Lord Maken. He mouthed silently to Mearns, 'Drunk, too much wine. You know how it takes the King sometimes.'

Mearns nodded. Scenes like this were not uncommon. He was not always involved. It was part of Castle life that was not often talked about.

'I haven't finished with Major Mearns,' was the answer. 'But I'm not quite sure what I want.'

'You will remember, Your Majesty,' said Lord Maken.

'Would you like me to come with you, Your Majesty?' said Mearns politely, hoping the offer would not be accepted.

The King went quiet for a moment.

'Later,' he said finally. 'I will see you get a message.'

*   *   *

Two days passed.

'He may have forgotten all about it,' said Denny. 'He's a funny fellow.'

'He usually remembers what he wants and, being who he is, usually gets it.'

*   *   *

The King was dressed in one of his sombre dark suits. In a low voice he said a name. 'Mrs

Fitzherbert. I want you to kill my wife.'

Major Mearns sat quietly, then he said, 'Yes, Mrs Fitzherbert is your wife.'

CHAPTER TEN

Charlie had heard what the Major said but he did not know what it meant. Who was Mrs Fitzherbert? And how could she be the King's wife? He already had a wife and a daughter, married and about to give birth.

He took himself off for a cup of coffee, which he was training himself to like.

He would not go to Ralli's, which even to his simple palate served the best coffee, because it was too expensive. Moreover, he might meet there the people he did not wish to meet while picking up information about the King and Mrs Fitzherbert.

So he went to a quiet little place, a mere hole in the wall, which he knew.

He slid into a seat at the back, close to where old Mrs Cheasle usually sat when she wanted a drink—which was often but, as she owned the place, no one stopped her.

He fumbled in his pocket, just enough for a cup of her weak coffee. Sometimes if she was in a good mood and felt generous she cut the price a fraction. On this day, however, she gave him a not unfriendly look before going back to drink her own tea.

Finally, he decided to ask her outright.

'Do you know Mrs Fitzherbert?'

Mrs Cheasle looked surprised. 'Not to say

"know".' She took a quick swig of her tea. Mrs Cheasle was an eccentric figure even in this Windsor hole. Charlie thought of it as a hole because it was down a flight of steps and underground. It had a kind of cosiness though, and it was cheap.

'Does she live in Windsor?'

There was a pause. 'I might have seen her here once. I think it was her—we all thought it was her . . . Why?'

'I wondered if she lived in the Castle.'

Mrs Cheasle said thoughtfully: 'If she did live in Windsor it would be in the Castle, I suppose, although she was seen in a house by the Theatre. I heard she was long gone, though.'

'Not dead?'

'Oh no, not dead; we'd have heard about her dying.' She sounded almost regretful.

'Oh, would you,' thought Charlie.

'Why?' he asked hopefully. There was something here he wanted to know. From what he had observed of Mrs Cheasle, he guessed she had plenty to tell him.

She gave him a hint now. 'We used to say—how was it?—her husband fell off his horse when he was riding home and killed himself.'

'Did he?'

'So we heard.'

'Wonder how much she makes up?' he thought, 'or embroiders?'

Mrs Cheasle gave him a long, thoughtful, but not ill-humoured look.

'She's enjoying this,' he thought. 'Well, if she can, then I can too. I must remember when I start writing.'

148

It was amazing, and puzzling, and deeply satisfying how his life was opening up in front of him.

His father would be pleased to see him back, even if it meant asking for some money so he could pay for some schoolwork. But he could imagine his mother's face; she would not be happy, as she had thought he was off their hands—no great career, but earning his own living.

He could understand it; she had carried him around for nine months, then given birth, and then fed him and trained him in the ways of the world, yet he had never felt any love there.

The interesting thing was that he suspected she would treat him exactly the same when he was rich and famous (as he was determined to be) and he respected her for that.

He sat in thought for several minutes. Not everyone had a mother whom they did not like and who did not much like them, but he must come to terms with it.

'I will buy her a present.' He had very small savings from his work in Windsor. 'A present from Windsor.'

'But what?' he grinned. 'I can't afford a crown.'

*   *   *

At the bottom of the Castle hill there was a small square of shops, next to the church and facing old Windsor—which was there back in the Anglo-Saxon times, decades before Norman William came blasting over the water from France.

Charlie had not known this before he came to Windsor, but he had been told it by Major Mearns

149

who, although he was a Royal servant, was not averse to making it clear that there was an England—and a rich and settled one—before the present Royal House.

It was the Major who took him round the shops, advising him what to use: 'When you've got any money,' with one of his large smiles; but he knew that, one way or another, Charlie had managed to earn something, even if not much.

'I like to earn when I can,' admitted the boy.

'And why not!'

There was a shop that sold silks and velvets in lovely colours—such lovely colours that he imagined the ladies of the Court shopping here, but he had never seen one go in there and come out with a bundle. For that matter, he had never seen anyone go in, let alone come out having shopped. But the shop had an air of quiet prosperity.

Suddenly he knew; this was theatre stuff—not for women to wear for everyday life, but on the stage, in a play; men too in some plays—say, Shakespeare.

He longed to touch and stroke the silks, but he also knew that he could not afford to, or not yet. Some time in the future—oh yes, he intended he should!

Next door was a smaller shop still, which sold the most delicious sweetmeats and chocolates. The Major had taken Charlie in and bought some chocolate. The owner of the shop, a man of kind heart, saw Charlie and came out to him.

'Here—try one of these.' He held out a handful of bright green balls. 'I had them sent to me from Scotland. They are called Soor Plums.'

Charlie put a ball in his mouth. It seemed to bite a hole in his tongue, but at the same time he liked it. He could tell that you could get fond of Soor Plums, acidic though they were.

As he stood there, sucking away, a small tabby cat sidled up beside him, and then went into the shop.

'Oh, there you are, Grissy,' said the shop man. 'Thought I'd lost you.' He looked at Charlie and smiled. 'Only joking. She doesn't go far.'

Charlie looked at the cat, which had a certain plumpness about its figure.

'She eats well—plenty of rats round here.'

But Charlie was a worldly-wise little Londoner. He smiled at the man and cocked his head sideways.

'Oh yes.' It came with a sigh. 'You're right. Another litter.'

'What will you do with them?'

'Oh, there's always the river.'

'No! You don't mean it. You couldn't . . .' Charlie paused; he didn't want to say the words.

There was a sigh, or perhaps a groan. 'No, I never have yet, but it gets harder to find good homes. Fortunately, she has very small litters. I have wondered if she eats some of them.'

'Surely not!'

'She might drop one or two in the river.'

Charlie could not believe it.

'It's what animals do,' said the man. 'Want another sweet?'

But Charlie was still sucking the bright green ball. Soor Plums were both powerful and long lasting.

'Lovely stuffs in the shop next door,' he

commented. He had a good view from where he stood of the velvets and silks in the window.

'You can go in and have a look round if you like. It's my shop.'

'Is it?' said Charlie with surprise. 'I would love to, if you are sure.'

Dombey and Son, said the name above the door.

'Dombey was my father. He left me the shop. I'm the son.'

Not sure if he was being laughed at or not, Charlie agreed he would like to go in. 'Seems a good name.'

'Mostly sold to Theatre folk.'

Charlie gave himself a mental pat on the back for getting it right.

'Not that they pay their bills,' said the Son of Dombey. 'Or not very fast. Just go in and look. Door's not locked. Don't touch though.'

'No, I won't. Thanks, Mr Dombey.'

'He has got a theatrical look at the back of the eyes himself,' thought Dombey. 'Be an actor himself, I wouldn't wonder, when he grows up. He has grown up already, in a way.'

'Did you ever see Mrs Fitzherbert?'

Dombey was surprised. 'What made you think of her?'

'Someone mentioned her.'

'I saw her once. She didn't come to the Castle much—or, if she did, she was kept hidden; that's how kings manage things. She may have lodgings here. A lovely lady; she'd have made a beautiful queen. Some people say he did marry her, but I don't know about that. We see and hear more in Windsor than is realised.'

'So do we in London,' thought Charlie.

As he wandered round the shop, Charlie wondered if Miss Fairface had been in here. Then to his great pleasure he saw her walking down the road. He wondered if she was coming into the shop where he was. But her eyes moved forward, further down the street—not into the sweet shop either; Miss Fairface was very careful about what she ate. But no, she was looking in the window of the jewellery shop. Yes, she liked to glitter; he had noticed that already.

Then he saw Felix coming down the road.

'I hate that man. I'm sure he would mistreat Miss Fairface if he got the chance, and I know he mistreats Spike and the dog. I'm going to rescue that boy before I go from here and if I can't do it myself I know who can; I shall ask Major Mearns.'

Then Felix stopped and looked straight at Charlie's face. For a moment he hesitated between him and Miss Fairface, then she marched on, undisturbed, towards the jewellery shop and Felix came towards the boy.

Charlie did not like the look in his face. He thought, 'I knew he didn't like me, but that look says he wants to hurt me. I must get the dog and boy away from him.'

Charlie stepped backwards into the black velvet hanging in folds. He peered out.

'Trying to see how you will look when you die?' said Felix grimly.

Charlie just stared, trying not to feel frightened.

For a whole minute they remained there, eye-to-eye, then Miss Fairface half-turned her head and gave a smile to Felix. He at once shot after her, smiling back. Miss Fairface went into the goldsmith's and Felix followed her.

'You fool!' thought the cynical young Londoner. 'She's an actress and will follow the rules of the world. She can smile and take, and give nothing back except her smile. But she will do it so gently and politely that you won't know what she's doing. You think you are clever and worldly wise, Felix, but Miss Fairface is in a way you would not understand.'

The pair were still in the goldsmith's shop. Charlie decided it might be sensible for him to get out from behind the velvets in case Miss Fairface fancied doing some shopping here.

He walked briskly out, and waved cheerfully at the kind donor of the sweet, which was still in his mouth, stuck to his teeth.

He knew he must go and talk to the boy before he did anything else. And talk to the dog; he might be able to tell the dog what to do if the boy got in trouble. The dog might be the more sensible one of the two.

*   *   *

Major Mearns was sitting in his room in the Castle, comfortable in his big armchair with a dog at his feet and a cat on his lap. He was drinking a glass of good burgundy, of which there was always plenty in the Castle cellars as it was the King's favourite wine too.

'Where did this cat come from?' he asked Sergeant Denny, who was sitting on an upright chair at the window.

'Walked in. Took a fancy to you and stayed. The dog you've always had.'

'I know that,' said Mearns irritably.

'He might have brought in the cat. They seem friendly.'

The Major looked with doubt at the friends. 'Perhaps Mindy knows something about the creature.' He did not dislodge the cat, but gave it a gentle stroke as he thought of Charlotte Minden.

'Anyway, you can ask her yourself.' Denny, from his window seat, had seen her arriving.

Mindy knocked on his door and walked in.

Mearns took his hand off the cat. 'Is this your cat, Mindy?'

'No, of course not. I don't have a cat.'

'You can have this one.' But the Major knew the cat was here to stay. He would have to find a name for him—*if* it was a 'him'—but, yes, this creature was surely male.

'Felix Ferguson has been calling on me these last weeks,' she announced. 'Oh, don't worry, he only wanted to talk—about himself, mostly. He thinks it makes me admire him.'

'No judge of a woman's nature,' said Denny. 'He never was. Knew his type in the army.'

'Today is Miss Fairface's turn,' Mindy announced. 'I saw them going into a shop near the Castle.'

'Miss Fairface is tougher than he realises,' said the Major. 'She knows how to take and not to give.'

Denny said in a firm voice: 'I think Ferguson is a cruel and violent man. I think he beats that boy he looks after, the dog too, I daresay. I saw blood on his stick. Dried blood, but blood and plenty of it.'

'He ought to be beaten himself,' said Mindy.

'You wouldn't do it yourself though, would you Mindy?' said the Major. He knew that, although Mindy was a successful Castle worker, much

155

appreciated by the people—all high-ranking—that she worked with, she came from a poor London background where you met violence with violence and knew how to defend yourself. She had come to the Castle a wild-eyed thin young girl as servant to Miss Fanny Burney. Miss Burney had hated Castle life as Lady-in-Waiting to a Royal princess, but Mindy was clever and had learnt from Fanny how to behave.

'No,' said Mindy, and the Major thought, with some amusement, that she said it with reluctance. 'No, my hands aren't strong enough. He's stronger than he looks, is Ferguson.'

'So she's had a brush with him,' thought the Major. 'Wonder what he tried on. What did he do to you? And what did you do to him? What a girl you are! I do love you, Mindy!'

To his surprise, he found he meant it.

When Mindy left a few minutes later, having delivered the laundry she had done for them (as she explained to them, she could no longer bear the sight of a badly ironed shirt), the Major knew he had lost his heart for ever.

He looked around for Denny to talk to, but he was nowhere in sight.

*   *   *

Charlie was speeding through the streets. When he got to the boy's house he hoped that Felix Ferguson was not yet home, but he thought he could tell from the expression on the dog's face that he was not. The Crowner was one of those people to whom animals responded at once, and not kindly.

Charlie climbed in through the back window and looked around for Spike.

He found him lying on the floor in the hall, his back against the wall. There was a long blue bruise down the side of his face.

'Did he do that to you?'

The boy nodded.

'All right,' said Charlie, 'I'm going to take you away. Gather up what you want to take.'

The boy got together his small pathetic traps: a broken comb, a white cotton square with ragged edges—obviously his handkerchief—and a battered, small, black notebook. Charlie, although not tall, was strongly built. 'Hop on my back. I'll help—hang on. Here we go. Come on Dog!'

The strangely assorted trio climbed the hill to the Castle. Charlie knew an entrance at the side and went through. He put the boy down on a chair, which was in a recess and used by the messengers. He stood beside him, resting a little after his exertions, with the dog crouched at his feet.

As soon as he had recovered his breath, Charlie said, 'Come on. Let's go and find the Major.'

Charlie knew how to get in, whether the Major was there or not. The door gave before him and the three of them were in.

No Major Mearns.

'What's all this?' demanded a voice from the door. Major Mearns stood there, looking stern.

'They're homeless,' said Charlie. 'There's lots of rooms in this Castle. I've seen them. No, I know what you are going to say: they are not yours to fill. But the King would not want this pair to be homeless.' Charlie added with a grin: 'And he need never know. I don't suppose he goes round all the rooms.'

'Kings get to know more than you might think,' said the Major, but he did not sound worried.

They were all surprised when Mindy and Denny came into the room together.

'We hear you've got another dog here.' This was Mindy.

The Major groaned. 'You can't keep anything quiet in this place.'

'I'm not against dogs,' said Denny, 'I like them.'

'The King wouldn't say anything. He's got half a dozen dogs himself. Anyway, there's no reason for him to know.'

'We won't tell him,' said Mindy. 'But someone else might.'

'He's only here until I can find a proper home for him. And for the boy,' said Charlie. 'They were with a man who used to beat them,' he explained.

'You'd better leave the boy and dog here. That's what castles are for, isn't it? To shelter those in need?'

Charlie looked thoughtful, but he understood what the Major was doing. 'Trust me', he seemed to be saying.

'So what do we call the boy?' he went on. 'We don't want this man to know they're here.'

Charlie looked at the Major and understood that he knew exactly who Spike and 'the man' were. He studied the boy and made his own decision. 'Jo.'

'And the dog?'

'Tom.'

The boy shook his head, tapped his breast and said: 'Tom', then pointed at the dog: 'Jo.'

'Sorry,' said Charlie, surprised. 'Got it wrong,

did I? You are Tom and he is Jo.'

'And what are you to be called, Charlie?' questioned an amused Major, wanting to bring him in on the game.

'Charlie!' he said fiercely. 'I am Charlie.'

'And,' he added in his mind, 'I will be famous one day, and everyone will know my name.'

The Major, guessing he had hit a sensitive point in the young rescuer, offered soothingly: 'I daresay you could stay here too, if you like—tuck you away beside the dog and boy.'

Unsure if that was a real offer or a joke, Charlie shook his head. 'No, of course I will come in and see them both, but I will stay in the Theatre—I like it there.'

Both the boy and the dog saw him go with calm faces.

'I'll be coming back for you, remember!' he said from the door. 'And you'll both be coming to London with me when I go.'

*　　　*　　　*

The Theatre always felt welcoming to Charlie. It wasn't that actors were always happy, but they knew how to ride out the ups and downs of life. And he felt they were teaching him.

All the same, he had no intention of going into adult life as an actor. He could already tell what he was going to do and it meant more education than he had now. It meant going back home and demanding it from his father. He thought his father would do his best—might even be pleased.

Sometimes the Theatre was busy with people rushing around with cheerful faces, and sometimes

159

all was quiet. Today was a quiet day.

Without surprise Charlie saw a mouse run across the floor in front of him. It looked a plump, well-nourished mouse and this did not surprise him either. He would not have been surprised to see a rat; there was plenty to eat in the Theatre, and mice and rats went where the food was. Miss Fairface had told him she had once seen a fox.

Charlie would have liked to see a fox. He sat down on a bench wondering if one would come along if he waited. And how long would he have to wait!

Miss Fairface came in carrying her make-up bag over one arm. This in itself was something he saw in his everyday life, although he could not imagine his mother with one.

'You all right?' asked the actress.

'Yes, just wondered if I would see a fox like you did. If I sat here quietly.'

'You might. What will you do if you do see one?'

'Just look, I expect.'

'I don't expect he'd bite—be more frightened of you than you were of him.'

'That's when animals bite,' said Charlie. 'Humans bite too.'

Miss Fairface looked at him thoughtfully. 'You're growing up very fast, Charlie.'

'I am going back to London.'

'I think I'm surprised you left, Charlie,' said Miss Fairface with a smile. 'You seem such a natural Londoner. So you're going? Any special reason?'

'I think it has something to do with that growing up.'

'I won't ask why.'

'I think I had better—I mean, ask myself why I'm going. I don't think Felix Ferguson will be pleased with me . . .'

'I wanted to warn you about that, Charlie, and also to ask you to help me find Henrietta's murderer.'

'Do you think it's Felix?'

'Who is that woman—or man—who was here and gave you the basket?'

'I don't know who it was, I didn't see the face under the bonnet, but I saw her dress and shawl in Felix's house,' whispered Charlie.

'He's got plenty of enemies, don't you worry! I wouldn't call him the most popular man in Windsor.'

'No,' said Charlie thoughtfully.

'There's a tale that he killed a young girl who worked in the Theatre and buried her under the floorboards here.' Miss Fairface looked around her as if she might pick out the actual board.

'Didn't anyone look to see?' Charlie was both surprised and shocked. Perhaps it wasn't true; it sounded like a made-up tale.

'I suppose the manager back then didn't want to find anything. Anyway, he died himself soon after.'

Yes, Charlie found it an interesting story! Theatre people were great storytellers, he had noticed. That did not mean they believed them, they just enjoyed doing it. He had noticed the pull himself. Easy and enjoyable to be a storyteller.

Miss Fairface got up from the bench to leave, saying she had to rest before the performance that evening. She disappeared from Charlie's sight, but he could still hear her talking to someone. 'Probably Ally Anderson, the wardrobe mistress,' he thought, but at first he wasn't sure; Miss Fairface was much easier to hear. Actresses learn to project their voice, Miss Fairface had told him.

But, yes, that sharp, low mutter *was* Mrs Anderson. She had a sharp tongue too when it suited her, but it was a stupid soul who quarrelled with a woman who made a good cup of tea like she did, and Charlie never did; and he noticed that Miss Fairface never did either.

He smiled. He knew a bit more about Miss Fairface than when he had first come to Windsor. She was friendly, but with more men friends than women; and she preferred a comfortably placed businessman or lawyer, rather than an actor.

'Money!' thought the cynical boy. One day she would marry (if she wasn't married already—he kept an open mind there), but then it would be to an actor. Performers had to marry performers. She had said that to him herself. He had told Major Mearns what she had said, and he had nodded. 'Oh yes, it's like being a Royal; you have to marry a Royal or it doesn't work. They're different sorts, you see.' He had added thoughtfully: 'Just as the rogues, thieves and killers who come in and out of my life are different and born that way.' He looked appraisingly at the boy. 'And you are a different sort, Charlie. I didn't see it at first, but I see it now. Or perhaps you are just growing into it.'

Charlie did not smile, for this was a serious matter. He felt there was something important inside himself like the seed of a plant.

You had to admit it with the Major; he could put his finger on it sometimes.

*   *   *

162

Charlie left the issue of his destiny undecided for the time being. It needed some thinking about. Meanwhile, a body had to be found.

'That floor looks difficult. How would I get it up? Or where to start?'

He began to pace the floor of the entrance hall, pondering the possibilities.

'You might kill a person in the entrance of a Theatre, but it's not easy to bury a body there.'

Charlie walked around thoughtfully. He couldn't see anything on the floor that hinted that it had been dug up. He couldn't think of anywhere else to look except that little wash place and lavatory no one used because it stank so.

Stank . . . smelt . . . A body would smell!

He had smelt one once before when, as a small boy, his family had moved to a house near a cemetery. The cemetery had been a little bit casual about burying its dead. His mother had soon moved them out of that house saying she knew why the rent was so low.

Charlie walked up and down outside the door, but he did not go in.

'What are you up to?' said a voice behind him. It was Fred, the stage set helper (he only carried in the furniture; the producer preferred his own assistants to do more—or even did it himself).

'Just poking around, Fred,' said the boy.

'Well, don't poke.'

Fred, who had good days and bad days, was clearly having one of his bad days. Charlie did not like the man. He had seen him beating a dog, but as the dog promptly bit Fred, who retired bleeding and shouting, the dog had got the better of the

163

clash. He turned out to be the live-in pet of the owner of the nearby ale-house where Fred would certainly not find himself welcome.

'Hear me there? Leave things alone!'

Charlie did not answer. He recoiled from Fred—and not only because of what he had done to the dog that day; there were other things which the boy did not dwell on.

Passing Fred on his way out, Charlie gave him a brief nod, but got nothing back.

He walked down the hill away from the Theatre. Tonight there would be a performance of *A Midsummer Night's Dream*. Miss Fairface was playing the Queen of the Fairies.

He didn't hear anyone behind him, but he must have been conscious of movement because he began to turn round to see a shadow looming over him.

Then something hard hit his head and he fell to the ground.

*   *   *

'You were lucky,' said Major Mearns.

'Doesn't feel like it.' Charlie rubbed his head. 'No blood anyway.'

'If Denny and I hadn't come down from the Castle to get a drink at that little ale-house beyond the Theatre, you'd be dead. He was trying to strangle you but he ran off when he heard us coming.'

'Or heard me,' said Miss Fairface. 'I was there too.'

'You were, ma'am, you were, but Denny and I are stronger. You might have got done yourself.'

Miss Fairface blinked. 'I'd have managed,' she said at last. But inside herself she was thinking that perhaps, after all, she was glad she had not got there in time to do anything.

Charlie struggled to sit up. 'I want to know who did it.'

The Major pushed him back down. 'Lie down.'

He looked at Denny, both of them exchanging the conviction of their suspicion about 'who did it'.

Charlie suddenly realised where he was—on the big, long chair in the Major's sitting room in the Castle. Staring at him with eyes of sympathy were the dog and the boy.

'You've got the lot of us,' said Charlie.

'So I have,' agreed the Major, but in no unfriendly way.

Charlie found that, while he was unconscious, his mind had been at work and come to a decision.

'I'll take us all away to London tomorrow.'

'How will you do that, lad?'

'I've got a bit of money. I saved it. It was what I was working for.'

'But London . . . ?'

'You can do anything in London,' said Charlie with conviction.

'London?' said Major Mearns. 'Yes, it might be wise for you to get away there. I can get you a seat on the coach and see you right for money. I hope you know your way around?'

*   *   *

There are so many Londons. Charlie knew this, but he knew too that *your* London was the one you lived in. That way you could have, of course,

165

several Londons, because the true Londoner liked to be on the move. But not outside a certain area.

He couldn't count himself as a Londoner as he had not been born there, and might not stay there; but he would think about it often and visit it often.

The dog and the boy would be a problem, but he had taken them over so he must look after them. He thought about the two of them and knew he could not let them down. Felix Ferguson would be looking for them. It could have been Felix who hit him on the head. Would he ever know?

More likely to have been the Theatre man, but he was not going to name him or ask. Just get away. He had never meant to stay in Windsor for ever; he had just been venturesome and felt it was a place he ought to see. He had seen it and liked it a lot. He would be back. But now he knew he must go.

Go to London.

CHAPTER ELEVEN

Charlie had arrived in London with Tom and Jo, thanks to Mearns' help, and they were lodging in a small but clean house that the Major had insisted was safe for them till he came to see them. Tom was happy and Jo was finding life full of surprises and kindness. Tom had a job working in a stables where Jo was allowed in, and where he caught rats with great regularity. Charlie strolled about, absorbing this new western side of London. One day he saw the elegant red-headed man who Mindy had told him was a Lord-in-Waiting.

Charlie was not surprised when the Major arrived with Denny in tow. He had somehow expected that Major Mearns would want to know how he and Tom were getting on. The Major arrived in the morning on a bright spring day, although there was a suggestion of rain in the air.

'You didn't come all the way to London just to see me?'

'And the boy. And the dog.' He smiled. 'All well, I see.'

Charlie nodded. 'Better than I would have expected.'

'London suits him. And the dog. But we miss him in the Castle.'

'He'd come back to Windsor, I daresay,' said Charlie thoughtfully. He himself might want to move on elsewhere, Charlie thought, and Tom and Jo might be able to come with him. 'If you made him a good offer!' he added.

Denny said that he missed them both and would be glad to have them both in the Castle.

'But what was it you came for?' asked Charlie.

'You know the ways of the Castle,' replied Major Mearns. 'I came to deliver a letter from the King by hand. I am on my way there now.'

Charlie said, with no question in his voice, 'To Mrs Fitzherbert.' Then he added, 'Can I come with you?'

He meant to go, having made up his mind at once. The Major knew this.

*　　　*　　　*

Mrs Fitzherbert had a house in Tilney Street, not far from Bond Street. It was an aristocratic, smart area, but the house was not large.

Although where Charlie had a room was certainly not aristocratic, it was within walking distance of Tilney Street.

The Major pulled the bell chain. The door was opened by a maidservant, and he went in.

'You don't go in with him?' Charlie said to Denny; they were watching from some way off.

'Not wanted.'

Charlie absorbed this information in silence for a moment, and then said, 'You come here though?'

'Yes, Charlie, yes, because after this we shall go off and have a drink and meet a few friends. It is an escape from the Castle. Yes, I know; you liked it, and so do I—but not all the time.' Denny paused for a moment.

'And Mindy's away,' he added morosely. 'She's gone off with Princess Augusta and one of her Ladies-in-Waiting to Bath.'

'And you miss her,' said Charlie with sympathy.

'We both do. She does our washing apart from anything else. She cooks our supper too sometimes.'

'I thought you got it from the kitchens, or you cooked.'

'Oh, yes, that is something that life in the army does teach you—how to cook when you have to. But a woman is better, you know . . . But Mindy is due back soon.'

The door of the house opened and the Major came out. Behind him came a woman who must have been Mrs Fitzherbert. She seemed to be talking in a forceful way to Mearns, whose face was impassive.

'He's not getting a pat on the back,' Charlie

decoded from what he saw, 'but a slap on the hand.' Then: 'An interesting face,' he thought. 'The sort of face that would get people writing about it. Not me, though.'

'What did he come here for?' Charlie asked Denny.

'Sent.'

'Oh? Why?'

Denny shrugged. 'I don't know exactly why, but the King sends him every so often. She's his wife.'

'Not the *King's* wife?'

'Yes. They were married years ago.'

Charlie studied the woman. 'She's very fat, but the face is beautiful—her skin gleams.'

'Yes, and it's natural—not like the King; his face is covered with grease and paint.'

'I noticed he looks a bit done over,' said Charlie, then: 'She looks as though she is being very sharp with the Major.'

'Be over money,' said Denny. 'Usually is; she wants more.'

'Well . . .' began Charlie thoughtfully.

'The King gives her ten thousand a year.'

Charlie was silenced. He could hardly believe it.

'But it's never enough,' Denny went on.

'How do you and the Major know all this?'

'Oh, we get to know most things.'

Major Mearns had made a slight, polite bow to Mrs Fitzherbert and then turned away. After all, the bow said, if things had gone differently she would have been his queen.

Perhaps she was the real wife, as she had certainly been the first one. 'Queen Fitzherbert,' thought the Major. 'What was her first name?' He found he did not know. Yes, he did: he

169

remembered it was Maria Anne.

He saw that Denny and Charlie were there too.

'You waited.' It was not a question.

'We wanted to see how you got on,' commented Denny.

'Oh, I got on,' replied the Major. 'A message to pass on to His Majesty. She made it clear what I was to say.' He looked around and asked Charlie: 'How's the lad?'

'Oh, he's working—takes it seriously. When it's work time then he works. Tom has changed— become more . . .' Charlie hesitated. 'Well, more solid is the word I think.'

'The dog too?'

Charlie considered. 'Yes, and Jo too.'

'You can all come back to the Castle with me if you desire.'

Charlie said thoughtfully: 'Give us another two weeks or so; he's learning so much.'

But really Charlie said this because he was worried about what Felix Ferguson would do. He did want to be there to see for himself.

However, this was not the only reason to hold back for a couple more weeks so that Tom and Jo could develop.

The perplexing thing was that Charlie could not be sure if he wanted to be there to protect Tom and Jo, or if he wanted them there to protect him.

CHAPTER TWELVE

As the little party waited in the inn courtyard for the Windsor coach, Mearns was looking with some amusement and pride at his young protégés. Charlie and Tom were washed and clean, and dressed in neat suits and boots, and the Major had taken them to the barbers in Covent Garden where the two boys had been given smart haircuts, whilst he had had a shave. The boys had washed the dog, who seemed to find this new experience enjoyable and fun, and Jo now had a proper collar to wear. Denny saw Mearns' look: 'You've taken a very fatherly view of our young team,' he grinned.

'They're going to be more useful than we realised,' replied Mearns. 'We must keep them safely with us till we solve our latest Windsor murders.'

The coach rumbled into the inn yard, and the ostlers ran to change the horses. The driver was the one who had first brought Charlie to Windsor, which seemed like years ago. He recognised Charlie. 'Well, young Sir. You have come up in the world!' Then turning to the Major: 'He does you credit, Sir.'

'Thank you. Tell me, whilst we are waiting, when you brought him here to Windsor, you kindly let him earn some money by bringing up two heavy parcels to me at the Castle. Did the ostler tell you who had given them to him?'

'He said it was a very tall, very thin woman—like Miss Tux who came down with us that day.' The coachman recollected: 'He did say this woman fair gave him the creeps. There was something he didn't like about her—"proper bullying type" he called her.'

'If it was a "her",' muttered the Major.

The coachman stared. 'That might explain the big hands he saw. Came from near the Theatre, too.'

Charlie heard all this without letting the men see he was listening. He was being cautious. He had been attacked. He had seen Mindy nearly burnt to death. He remembered the chef and the actor who both had strange affectionate ways. Could women kill? Could a woman killer cover her tracks? Could she kill again?

Charlie pondered these matters on the very comfortable journey inside the coach—to the Windsor he knew was now becoming more and more important to him. On arriving at the inn yard there, he noticed it was the same ostler as the coachman had pointed out to Mearns. Charlie asked him about the mysterious woman and the two heavy parcels.

The ostler told him she had been hanging around near the inn or near the Theatre for some time. The heaviness of the parcels hadn't seemed to worry her, and she had held them all the time as if they were valuable. Yes, he had noticed the large hands: 'Now you mention it, they could have been the hands of a man. That could explain why she just didn't seem right.'

Mearns and Denny took the two boys and Jo to the Castle, where they found them a room in which to sleep, and then gave them a good meal from the Royal kitchen. Then they brought them into Mearns' room for a talk.

172

Firstly, Charlie told the Major that he had seen the red-haired Lord near Mrs Fitzherbert's house in London. Then he explained about the privy at the Theatre, which no one used because of the awful smell—much worse than most privies. The Major sat up like a hound straining at the leash— enough to startle Jo who sat up with equal alertness.

'Yes, you can come with us too, Jo,' said Mearns. 'Dol killed in the dressing room. The attempt to kill Mindy—saved thanks to you, Charlie. The actress slain as well—or instead. The attack on you, dear boy . . . There's something rotten in the state of Denmark!—as the players might say.'

The two men, the two boys and Jo walked swiftly to the Theatre and entered the yard quietly. Charlie got the spade and Denny started digging by the privy in fits and starts. Although the Major scattered flowers around, and smoked a pipe vigorously, the smell was now even worse.

As he dug deeper into the earth, Denny gently dug in smaller spade-fulls. Soon clothes could be seen—a waistcoat, then the body of a headless and legless man. 'Traddles, poor devil! Get a wheelbarrow, Charlie. We must take him away. God be thanked the new mortuary attendant is one of my ex-soldiers, and an honest man. We'll not tell the Theatre they can use this privy again—not for the moment.'

They wheeled the body to the mortuary, having covered it with a sack. Jo was so interested in the whole proceedings that Mearns could not help thinking the dog was indeed proving to be a useful member of his team.

On the way back Charlie told the Major he felt

strongly it was Beau who had hit him, though he could not be sure why. They turned back to the Theatre and were lucky to find Miss Fairface in her dressing room—obviously relieved to see them. She informed them that Beau had been out of breath and very agitated when he had arrived at the Theatre that day. She also told them she was sure the 'creature' who had given Charlie the parcel near the Theatre was the same man or woman she had noticed in the green room at the time of the dressing room murder.

Charlie suddenly remembered that Willie, the ex-actor who knew Tosser, had seen the parcel being handed to him. They found Willie sitting in one of the nearby coffee shops with a small cup of coffee. Mearns immediately brought him another and a slice of ham to go with it. Willie's tongue was loosened by this unexpected sustenance, for which he was full of gratitude.

'I tell you, Sir, Tosser was a devious fellow— very devious! And looked not to the order of his going. One day I came up to sup with him, and as I reached his door I heard shouting. Tosser was demanding money, or he could make life difficult for the other man. Blackmail to my mind. Hoist the black flag and begin slitting throats!—my own words, from a speech I wrote.'

'What other man, did you see him?'

'That I did, Sir. I hid round the corner as he was coming out, and saw him striding away; but he didn't see me. It was Felix, the Crowner.'

As they were leaving, after giving a coin to Willie, Charlie told the Major that he had seen the man-woman's dress, shawl and bonnet hanging in the cupboard in Felix's house when he had climbed up to speak to Tom—or Spike—and Jo.

'Corruption—corruption! It's spreading like a stone thrown into a pond,' muttered Mearns. 'And how are we going to prove who is the spider lurking in the centre of this web?'

They decided to return to the mortuary to search for any clues left with the bodies.

'If Felix killed Dol, then who let him into the Theatre, and why did he kill her?' asked Mearns.

'Surely it must have been Henrietta,' offered Miss Fairface.

Mearns, who had been turning out the pockets of Tosser and Traddles, found a stained and crumpled note in Tosser's coat. It was signed F, fixing an appointment. 'Ha!' he exclaimed. 'Suppose Dol had been demanding money as well?'

Miss Fairface commented: 'Sometimes I could smell Dol on Beau when we were on stage together, and I taxed him about it.'

* * *

Back at the Castle, Mindy—who had returned from her trip to Bath—joined them for a glass of wine as she returned another of Denny's shirts. She offered to mend any of Mearns' shirts, and those of the two boys as well. Mearns smiled fondly at her, not unnoticed by Denny and Charlie.

Mindy questioned them so relentlessly that Mearns told her the whole story—not displeased to see the admiring look she gave him when he had finished.

'I think I can help you,' she said thoughtfully, and rather timidly. 'I will meet Felix. Let him think

I am, shall we say, not ignoring him, and see what he tells me—more importantly, what he does not tell me.'

Mearns regarded her anxiously. He noted her bright, intelligent eyes, her colouring, the elegant picture she made in another high-waisted blue dress that fitted her slim figure well.

'It won't be a risk. I will take Jo with me, and Charlie can keep in the background to watch over my welfare.'

Charlie and Jo sat up eagerly. Mearns caught Denny's eye—the thought in both their minds that they, too, would be in the vicinity. On that note of agreement they fixed a time for the morrow, in the morning.

* * *

The next morning Mindy and Jo, whose lameness was now cured, walked past Felix's office, pretending indifference, but hoping that he was in the front room. From out of the corner of her eye she saw Felix notice her and the dog, and she walked on. A few moments later she heard Felix running after her.

'Mindy, my dear, what brings you out this morning, and with this dog?'

'There is so much bustle and worry going on in the Castle, I cannot stand it, so I offered to go to the mantua-maker's, and took the dog for a walk.'

'What sort of bustle is going on?'

'Perhaps you have heard of it. Indeed perhaps you can set my mind at rest a little. They are all talking of Mrs Fitzherbert, and there are strange officers here now, and the most frightening rumours. Have you heard aught of it?'

Felix frowned and glared at her, then made a threatening gesture, at which she pretended to be so in fear that she and Jo ran away—not past Felix's house, but towards the town.

Charlie dodged down an alley behind the house to a sidestreet so that he was at the corner as she ran towards it. Mearns and Denny were hiding round the opposite corner. Meanwhile, Mindy had been letting all three of them know she saw them, with a flirtatious wink and smile.

Felix turned back to his own house, scowling furiously. By a roundabout way, past the mantua-maker's in case Felix was having Mindy followed, the party returned to the Castle. As they walked along Mindy gave them her impressions of Felix's words and demeanour.

Mearns pondered. 'So! Felix is worried about Mrs Fitzherbert. And we know that Lord Maken is visiting Mrs F in London—thanks to you seeing him there, Charlie. And Mrs F's message to the King, which I have not yet given him, is not what I thought a beleaguered woman would threaten.'

Charlie enquired, 'Sir, what about the house near the Theatre where Mrs Fitzherbert stayed?'

'We'll go round there now. 'Tis only a few yards out of our way, and we'll see what we can learn.'

On arriving there and finding the house empty, they called in on the neighbours and found out that it was only a rented house. They learnt that it was currently let to a Mr Montresor, a tall, red-haired man, with a very condescending air.

'Maken—or I'm a Dutchman!' grunted Mearns, slapping one fist into the palm of another. 'Now, why is he doing this? Is it a plot against Mrs F by the King?'

'Could it not be the other way round?' suggested Mindy excitedly. 'Can it be a plot against the King by Mrs F and Lord Maken, with Felix doing all their dirty work while they keep safely in the background?'

'Aye! And this must be why they sent me those bits of poor Traddles' body—to discredit me. But we beat them on that because we haven't let them know *all* we know. Good girl, Mindy. We'll make a Watcher of you yet!'

She blushed and lowered her eyes lest Mearns read too much in them. Mearns continued to ponder: 'Why should Beau visit Dol? Rather than any other ladies of the night? Is it because of who she knows? Or is it because of where she lives—on the top floor of that house, overlooking the Castle?'

'What about Henrietta's other lovers?' queried Denny.

*   *   *

Mearns left the others safely at the Castle, and walked back to the Theatre. Beau was in his dressing room, so Mearns was able to question him fiercely and searchingly—particularly about Dol, Felix and the attack on Charlie. He told Beau that he suspected that he had killed Dol before going on stage that night. And that Henrietta had dragged the body out of their hiding place before 'finding' her. Beau spluttered angrily but without conviction. Mearns left him red in the face and slipped into Miss Fairface's dressing room. He told her the position to date and was not surprised to learn that Henrietta did have other lovers besides her mysterious Lord, and also that she had been seen whispering with Felix. Miss Fairface offered to adopt the ploy of Mindy and make up to Lord Maken in order to see what he might let slip.

*　　　*　　　*

Next morning over a breakfast of Royal ham and coffee and a carefully held newspaper, Mearns and Denny summed up the case.

Denny reported to the Major: 'I have not been idle. I have learnt that Traddles had been heard to say he was on to something that would make his fortune, and give the Castle something to worry about; also, it was rumoured that it was Felix who killed and buried the baby found in the Theatre back yard. People say it was the offspring of Mrs Fitzherbert and Lord Maken, and that it was buried some time ago. They must have employed Felix to get rid of it. He's been doing their dirty work for them ever since, and buried Traddles's dog in the same hole. If it was so widely talked about in the Theatre, perhaps it was also heard in the town.' Mearns told Denny to make his usual quiet walk round the town after returning *The Times* to John, the King's top dresser. Meanwhile, he, the Major, would watch the Theatre.

*　　　*　　　*

A couple of hours later they met for a cup of coffee in a coffee house near the Theatre where Miss Fairface joined them. She told them Beau had not arrived for rehearsal.

179

'I'll tell you why,' reported Mearns. 'He was found with his throat cut in a back alley this morning, and is now in the mortuary. My guess is that he was so scared yesterday he went to somebody—Felix! Or who else?—and got killed for his pains.'

'But how did Beau get involved in the first place?'

'Perhaps he wanted to make his fortune. He must have been promised a lot of money for his help. He could keep an eye on both the Theatre and the Castle—through Dol's window. He was perfectly placed for them. But Dol must have suspected something was up and tried to blackmail him, and that's when he killed her.'

Miss Fairface nodded slowly, then said, 'I met Lord Maken and it was obvious he knew all about Mrs Fitzherbert. He had been sure all was going according to plan, but he got rattled when I told him you were planning an arrest today. He is very close to Mrs F. I am sure he is trying to get a message to her, and I think Felix must be the messenger.'

*　　　*　　　*

Later Mindy came to the room where the two boys and Jo were staying. She was wearing a long shawl. She motioned them to silence. 'I am going to the room where Tosser lived. I am taking Willie, the old actor, and will look for the money I am sure Tosser had blackmailed out of Felix and cheated out of his clients. Would you both like to come with me, and bring Jo? We should be safe enough together.' With that she brought her hand from below her shawl; she was holding a long, thin, and very sharp kitchen knife.

They set off across the courtyard quickly. They did not look up at Mearns' window, else they would have seen him staring after them. 'Where are they off to, Denny? I'll wager I know. They are going to search Tosser's room. Come, Denny, we must follow them to see them safe. Bring your pistol.' And, suiting action to the words, Mearns pocketed his own neat pistol in his coat, and they hurried after the party.

Mindy, the boys and Jo met Willie, and together they soon reached Tosser's room. Nothing had been touched or cleaned. 'Now, Willie, you've sat with him many times. Where would he hide his money? Nowhere very clever, because he wasn't one for thinking too deeply. I promise you, if we find it, after we return what money he stole or swindled you shall share with us.'

As Mindy spoke she was pouring water from a bucket over the mud floor and the bricks round the hearth to see where the water would make a depression, showing recent digging. As she saw the boys' wide-eyed stare, she explained, 'This is how they hide their money in the rookeries and stews of London.'

Willie said: 'I think you are right. I once arrived here quietly and found Tosser moving the bricks round the fireplace.' The water Mindy poured sank away, and the boys started pulling up the bricks, which came away with ease. Sure enough, there was a packet in oilskin. They opened it to find several letters, and a bag of gold coins.

Suddenly, they had company.

'You've saved me the trouble of looking, and

made it so convenient for me to make sure none of you will live to tell the tale,' said a sharp voice behind them. Felix came through the open door. He took from his belt a knife and started to walk towards them with his left hand held out ready for the packet.

Mindy drew her knife from under her shawl and, holding it in the way of professional killers, with the blade upwards, she stabbed Felix in the back of his left hand. He shouted, dropped his knife and, as he bent forward, Jo—who had been crouching low on the ground—leapt forward and crushed Felix's throat in his strong jaws, then held on despite the man's desperate struggles. Mindy then drove the knife into Felix's right hand as he sought to throw off the dog. As his struggles and gasps weakened, Mearns and Denny burst in, their pistols in their hands.

'Good boy, Jo!' gasped Mearns. He put a bullet carefully into Felix's heart. Jo let go when he was sure the quarry was dead, then sat proudly by the corpse, wagging his tail, as the boys stroked and cuddled him.

'Mindy! Are you all right? Did he hurt you? Why didn't you let me know where you were going, my dear?' He held her wrists firmly and spoke with a look in his eyes that betrayed his feelings to them all, not excluding Jo.

'We'll take this packet to the Coroner for him to find the owners and then I'll see you share what's left. Not Denny, nor me—we are just doing our job in the Castle.'

*   *   *

Over supper in Mearns' room the celebration was on several counts. The Coroner had agreed that Mindy, the boys and Willie would have a share in the treasure trove. Miss Fairface had told them that one of the managers of the Drury Lane Theatre, where her parents were playing, had come to Windsor to see her, and she was to go to London right away with Mr Thornton's blessing to undertake some small parts in the current bill there. And she had offered to take Charlie back with her.

Mearns was regarding Jo with a puzzled air: 'That dog is no stray, no wild dog,' he observed. 'He behaves like a well-trained dog. Has he always been yours, Tom?' The boy nodded happily. Mearns suddenly remembered. 'Where's that pocket-book you brought with you from Felix's house, when Charlie rescued you?'

Tom went to get it, and gave it to the Major, who studied the papers in it. After a few moments while they all watched breathlessly, he said triumphantly, 'Well, Tom, we know who you are! You're not Tom. You are Robert, and your father is Sir Robert Turner, the baronet who lives just outside Windsor, not far away from the Great Park, and I think . . .'

The boy interrupted him: 'Robert, yes. A house with wide steps, and a large garden, and hens and cows and horses—and my mother and my sister.' The floodgates of repression and fear burst, and he looked years younger, while Jo jumped up and down barking furiously.

Mearns shouted joyously: 'You were kidnapped for ransom by Felix! So tomorrow I will take you home to your father and mother—with Jo, of

183

course!'

'What about that Lord Maken and Mrs Fitzherbert?' asked Mindy, sitting next to the Major who was still holding her hand protectively.

'I explained to them what we knew, and what we could tell His Majesty. Lord Maken decided he would retire immediately to his estates in Ireland. He has already made his farewells and gone! And I think Mrs Fitzherbert will be living a quieter life from now on and will be content with whatever the King gives her.'

*   *   *

A couple of days later, with young Robert and Jo restored to the Turner family, Mearns, Denny and Mindy were sitting with Charlie, who was due to leave on the coach on the morrow.

Taking a letter from his breast pocket, Mearns said, 'I have news for you all. I have sent my report to Lord Castlereagh as usual, but Sir Robert has also contacted his Lordship. He has written to me, and offered me a knighthood. How would you like to be a Lady, Mindy? Denny and I will be settling permanently here in the Castle, but I shall be reporting to Milord, rest assured.'

Mindy blushed and smiled her pleasure whilst nodding eagerly.

Denny said, 'May I congratulate you, and say how happy I am—but not surprised, mark you!'

Mearns chuckled as he took a ring from his waistcoat pocket and slipped it on Mindy's finger. 'Well now, Charlie, tomorrow you go back to your parents in London. And I know your father, absent-minded though he be, will be pleased to see young Charlie returned to the family.'

Charlie stood up. 'Not Charlie any more. From now on I will always be known as Charles Dickens.'